"What were we talking  n started?" Deborah asked.

"Not we—you," Carole said. "You were talking about the time before we rode horses."

"That's it, then," said Deborah. "I don't want you to beat me at Scrabble with horse words. I don't want you to read to me from your horse books. I want each of you to tell me a real-life story that really happened to you."

"Great," said Stevie. "There was the time Belle and I—"

"No. I want to hear stories that don't have anything to do with horses."

"What for?" Carole asked.

"Well, my baby is going to be surrounded by horses and horse talk all of his life. Horses are fun, but they aren't everything. I'd like to know that somehow, something other than horses was ever important to the three of you. I've got to admit that I find the idea that I'm about to be a mother even scarier than the idea that I'm about to have a baby. So, I need some help. I know I can always get help from you about horses. Give me some help about mothering."

The girls looked at one another.

"No horses?" Carole asked.

"Not a one," Deborah said.

There was a long silence.

THE SADDLE CLUB
SUPER #5

BEFORE THEY
RODE HORSES

BONNIE BRYANT

A SKYLARK BOOK
NEW YORK • TORONTO • LONDON • SYDNEY • AUCKLAND

RL 5, 009–012

Before They Rode Horses

A Bantam Skylark Book/May 1997

ISBN 0-553-48376-5

Published simultaneously in the United States and Canada.

Bantam Books are published by Bantam Books, a division of Bantam Doubleday Dell
Publishing Group, Inc. Its trademark, consisting of the words "Bantam Books" and
the portrayal of a rooster, is Registered in U.S. Patent and Trademark Office and in
other countries. Marca Registrada. Bantam Books, 1540 Broadway, New York, New
York 10036.

PRINTED IN THE UNITED STATES OF AMERICA

OPM   0 9 8 7 6 5 4 3 2 1

In memory of my parents—
Metzer and Emmons Bryant—
who knew me
before I rode horses

"DON'T WORRY, MAX, we'll take care of everything," Stevie Lake said. She was talking to Max Regnery, the owner of Pine Hollow Stables and her riding instructor. "The whole place is in the hands of The Saddle Club!"

"That's what I'm afraid of," Max said. There was a twinkle in his eye, though. "If I leave you girls in charge, I never know what I'll find when I get back!"

Pine Hollow was the place Stevie and her two best friends, Carole Hanson and Lisa Atwood, loved best in the world because it was all about one thing: horses.

Stevie (short for Stephanie), Carole, and Lisa were three very different girls who had one very big thing in common. They loved horses. The girls loved horses so much that they'd formed The Saddle Club. The club had only two rules. Members had to be horse-crazy—that was the easy part—and they had to be willing to help whenever help was needed, even if the person getting help didn't know that they needed help.

In this case, the person they were helping *knew* he needed help. Max and his mother, called Mrs. Reg by all the riders, were going to a full-day Pony Club instructor's meeting and had to be away from Pine Hollow until late that night. The regular stable hand, Red O'Malley, was away at his girlfriend's college graduation. That left Max's wife, Deborah, in charge of the house and the stables.

There were two problems with that. The first was that Deborah didn't know much about horses. She was learning as fast as she could (with some help from The Saddle Club), but the amount she didn't know was much larger than the amount she did know.

The second problem was that Deborah was going to have a baby. The baby was due in another month. Although she'd had an uneventful pregnancy, she was very big and she didn't move easily. She'd definitely need help to look after the stable for a day. The Saddle Club had volunteered. They were trying to convince Max that he didn't have a thing to worry about.

"Look, have we ever let you down?" Lisa asked.

Stevie nudged her sharply. "Bad question," she whispered.

"Well . . . there was the time . . ." Max's voice trailed off.

"We fixed that before you got back," Stevie said hastily.

". . . and then I remember a certain bucket of paint . . ."

"It came out!" Lisa reminded him.

". . . and that time with the saddles . . ."

"Nobody was using those anyway!" Carole protested.

Max looked at his mother. "Maybe we'd better cancel," he said. He sounded serious, but the girls knew he was joking. Not only were they horse-crazy, but they were also horse wise, and Max knew he could trust them. He and his mother hugged Deborah and wished her good luck "in the hands of The Saddle Club." They waved as their car pulled out of the driveway.

3

They were almost to the road when Max put the car in reverse and backed up.

"Don't tell me you've changed your mind," Stevie said into the open window.

"No, I just remembered that I forgot to tell you that Judy is stopping by later on. I want her to take a look at Patch. He seems to be favoring his left hind foot," Max said.

"We'll keep an eye out for her," Carole promised.

Judy Barker was the vet who looked after all of Pine Hollow's horses. She had taught the girls everything they knew about equine health. She was a regular visitor to their Pony Club meetings and a great teacher.

Finally, the car pulled out of the driveway, turned onto the road, and kept going.

"Alone," said Deborah.

"At last!" said Lisa.

"I thought they'd never go," said Stevie.

"We've got some work to do," said Carole.

"So do I," said Deborah. "I've got an article to finish."

Deborah was an investigative reporter for a newspaper in nearby Washington, D.C. She sometimes went to her office, but more often these days, she worked from home, sending her articles into the paper straight from her computer.

The girls told Deborah they'd check on her when they were done with their chores. Deborah was more than happy to let them do the stable work while she took care of her own.

"There are four stalls that need mucking out," Lisa said. "We should do that first because it's the most unpleasant chore. Then we can give water and hay to all the horses. Then, Mrs. Reg left a note about some saddles that need soaping, and after that—"

"After that, we'll need a break," said Stevie. By "break," she meant a trail ride in the woods behind the stables. The girls liked everything about horses and riding, but they liked trail rides the best.

"Unless Patch needs some help from us," said Carole. They agreed to check on Patch before they went out on the trail.

In minutes, the three of them were all mucking out stalls. The girls were devoted to horses and didn't mind doing even the most unpleasant job, as long as it was for a horse. They agreed that riding was a privilege granted by the horse in exchange for caretaking. To them, mucking out a stall, wrapping a sore leg, or hauling a bale of hay was a very small price to pay for all the fun of riding.

It was typical of the three of them that Lisa had organized the work schedule, that Stevie had figured out when they'd start to have fun, and that Carole would remind her friends that their fun would begin only when they were sure they had done everything the horses could possibly have needed from them.

Lisa was the most organized of the three girls. Stevie sometimes teased her, saying that she probably dreamed in alphabetical order. Lisa told her she'd tried that once, but when she got to *h* for *horse,* she'd lost track of the alphabet. She was always neatly dressed, never made a mess and never seemed to get her clothes wrinkled. Her report card was very dull, according to Stevie, because it had nothing but As on it (Stevie's was often dangerously colorful, by comparison). Lisa was the oldest of the three friends, but she'd been riding for the shortest time. However, she was such an apt pupil at riding, as with everything else, that she was nearly as good as her two friends. Lisa's mother was of the opinion that a properly raised young lady had many skills, and as a result Lisa had taken lessons in dance, painting, music, and even knitting. It

6

seemed that no matter how many activities her mother loaded on her, Lisa always managed to do each of them well. But she liked riding the best and always found a way to make time for doing it with her two best friends.

While Lisa was an expert in everything she did, Carole focused all of her efforts on horses. Of the three girls, she was the horse-craziest. She'd known from the first time she'd been on a horse that all she ever wanted to do in her life was to be with horses. When she grew up, she'd work with them. Sometimes she thought she'd be a trainer. Then the next day, she'd decide to be a vet. Or maybe she'd be a show rider, or perhaps a breeder, or a trader, or maybe— She simply couldn't pick one. For now, she'd decided to be all of them.

While Carole never forgot a detail having to do with horses and their riding and care and stable management, she often forget details about the rest of her life. If she went on a trip, she always packed her riding clothes, but she might leave her toothbrush, nightgown, or shoes behind. When she left the house in the morning, she might leave her book bag on the kitchen table, but the backpack that held her riding gear never left her side!

Carole lived with her father, a colonel in the

Marine Corps. Almost all her life, she and her family had moved wherever the Marine Corps had sent them. It hadn't been easy on Carole or her mother, but they'd learned to adjust to their new homes. Then, finally, her father had been stationed at Quantico, outside of Washington, and they'd known this would be where they would stay for a long time. They'd bought a house—the first time they'd ever owned a house off a base—and they'd settled in Willow Creek. That was when Carole had started riding at Pine Hollow. It was a wonderfully happy time until Carole's mother had gotten ill with cancer. She had died of it soon after.

During her mother's illness and after her death, Carole had found that the only place she could be content was with horses. She somehow managed to put all her worry and sadness aside when she was in the saddle, concentrating completely on the one thing she could count on, the one thing that would never change in her life—her love of horses.

While Lisa was serious about everything and Carole was serious about horses, it sometimes seemed to the two of them that Stevie was serious about only one thing: fun. Stevie was famous for her weird sense of humor and her passion for pranks and practical jokes. Not everybody agreed with Stevie's idea of fun, and the result was that she spent a lot of time in hot water. That had merely honed her abilities to get out of it. Her teachers sometimes complained that she spent more time in the principal's office than she did in class. She assured everyone that that was a wild exaggeration and, if the principal would just listen more attentively while Stevie explained things, it wouldn't take nearly as much time.

Stevie's parents were both lawyers working in Washington. Stevie had three brothers: an older brother named Chad, a twin brother named Alex, and a younger brother named Michael. Being the only girl wasn't always easy, and Stevie often relied on her resourceful imagination to figure out how to get back at them when they teased her or played jokes on her. It didn't always make for peace at home, but—much to her parents' consternation— there was never a dull moment at the Lake household.

As Stevie had become expert at getting herself into trouble, she'd also gotten pretty good at taking her friends along with her. Carole and Lisa never knew what was going to happen when Stevie came up with one of her harebrained schemes. Stevie was fond of pointing out to them that, more often than not, her schemes worked. She had accomplished some pretty amazing things with her pranks and jokes. She'd also spent more time than she usually recalled being grounded for them.

The one thing the girls always agreed on was that they loved horses. Stevie and Carole each had her own horse. Carole's, a half-Thoroughbred bay gelding, was named Starlight for the nearly perfect six-pointed star on his forehead. Her father had given him to her for Christmas one year, and Carole was convinced he was the best Christmas present anyone could ever have.

Stevie's horse, Belle, was an Arabian-Saddlebred mix. She was sweet and spirited just like Stevie and even sometimes got into trouble. Belle had an allergy to certain weeds that seemed to taste good—at least to her—so whenever the girls rode, Stevie had to be sure Belle didn't get anywhere near temptation. Stevie was happy to do whatever was necessary to protect her beloved horse.

Lisa didn't own a horse. Part of her wanted badly to own one, but another part of her knew that she was still a relatively new rider, and it was good for her to have the experience of riding a lot of different horses. Most of the time, she rode a Thoroughbred mare named Prancer that belonged to the stable. Prancer had retired from the racetrack when she'd developed a weakness in her legs that had ended her racing career, but that didn't impede her quality as a hackney at Pine Hollow. Lisa was sure, too, that Prancer would make a great show horse eventually, and she was bound and determined to be the rider who won Prancer's first blue ribbon.

"Done!" Stevie called out from Nero's stall.

"Me too, almost," Lisa announced as she peered out the doorway of Prancer's stall. "I just have to make the bedding more even."

"I'll give you a hand," Stevie offered.

With a few quick, smooth strokes, the job was done. The girls led Prancer back into her fresh clean stall and latched the door.

"Why don't you bring in a bale of hay and distribute it while I clean Penny's stall?" Carole suggested.

The girls divided their tasks naturally and helped one another easily as they finished up the chores. When the last stall was clean and every horse and pony in the stable had fresh hay and water, the three of them went to check on Patch.

Patch was one of their favorite lesson horses. He was a black-and-white paint gelding that a lot of new riders started on at Pine Hollow. Carole clipped a lead line on his halter and patted his neck affectionately.

"Come on, boy, let's take a look at that foot of yours before Judy gets here."

Patch's ears perked up curiously as she talked. He always responded to kindness. It was one of the things that made him a favorite.

Carole tugged gently. Patch stepped gingerly out of the stall. Stevie watched his feet; Lisa watched his head and his ears; Carole listened.

There was no mistake about it. Something was wrong with his foot or leg. Lisa saw his ears go back when he put weight on the sore foot. Stevie saw him pull the foot off the floor as soon as he could transfer weight to his other feet. Carole heard Patch's uneven footsteps as he moved forward.

Stevie, Carole, and Lisa all knew that Max would have checked Patch for obvious problems before he'd called Judy, but they wanted to look for themselves. Carole held the lead line and comforted the ailing horse while Stevie and Lisa checked for sources of the problem. Stevie looked at Patch's hoof first. Sometimes a stone could get stuck under a horse's shoe. She ran her finger around the underside of the shoe and found nothing. She checked the bottom of his foot for soreness, but he didn't flinch, so she decided it wasn't a bruised frog. She felt his hoof and then his ankle for warmth, knowing that if there was infection, there might be inflammation. It felt all right to her, but to be sure, she also felt his other foot. It seemed to be the same temperature. She felt along his lower leg for any swelling. She didn't find anything. Then she checked the left leg against the right one just to be sure they were the same size.

"Beats me," she said finally.

"Then I guess it's a good idea that Judy's coming to take a look at it," Lisa said.

The girls decided that it might help Patch to put a wrap on the leg until Judy got there. At the very least, it wouldn't hurt, and it might make Patch more comfortable. Stevie got the bandage and Carole held Patch's lead while Lisa wrapped the leg.

"What a team we are!" Stevie said proudly when they'd finished taking care of Patch. "I think we can accomplish anything, as long as we work together."

"And as long as it has to do with horses," said Lisa.

Carole smiled at her two friends. "Okay, okay, enough of this work stuff. Did somebody say something about a trail ride a while back?"

It was time for some fun.

2

"WHY DON'T WE go see how Deborah's doing?" Lisa asked.

"Better still, why don't we see if Deborah would like to come along with us?" Stevie suggested.

"Great idea," Carole said.

They found Deborah sitting at her desk, glaring at her computer screen.

"Are we interrupting?" Lisa asked.

"I wish you were!" Deborah said. "I've been looking at this thing for an hour and absolutely nothing has come of it. I just can't figure out how I want to start my article. I'm totally stuck. Any ideas?"

"You bet," said Stevie. "Whenever I have trouble

14

thinking about what I want to do, I just go for a ride. How about that?"

"Yeah, we're going on a trail ride," Lisa said. "Would you like to come with us?"

"Like this?" Deborah asked, pointing to her enlarged belly.

"The doctor said you could ride, didn't he?" Carole asked.

"Oh, sure," Deborah said. "I'm just supposed to take it easy. No galloping, no jumping, no steeple-chasing."

"You never did that stuff *before* you were pregnant!" Lisa said.

"That was his point," Deborah said, grinning. "He told me that I could and, actually, *should* keep on doing everything I'd been doing before I became pregnant, and I guess that includes being a beginning rider. Do you really want to go on a trail ride with someone who can't go faster than a walk?"

"Yes!" said Lisa.

"I guarantee it'll help you think better," said Stevie.

"I'll tack up Delilah," Carole offered.

"I'll change my clothes and meet you at the good-luck horseshoe," said Deborah.

Fifteen minutes later, the four of them were ready

15

to ride. Before they left, they each touched the stable's good-luck horseshoe. According to tradition, no rider at Pine Hollow who touched the horseshoe had ever been seriously hurt in a riding accident. Some of the younger riders thought that meant the horseshoe had magic powers. The older riders suspected that touching the shoe was a way to remind riders that they needed to be careful. Whatever the cause, the effect was a good one. Safety was the first rule of riding at Pine Hollow, and the girls were determined to make this a safe ride for Deborah.

They rode four abreast across the fields as they headed for the woods.

"I've been thinking about a horse," Carole said.

"You're always thinking about horses," said Lisa.

They all laughed because they knew that was true.

"Well, more specifically, I've been thinking about Patch," she said. "I wish I could figure out what's wrong with him."

"He's got a sore foot. That's what Max said," Deborah told them.

"Ah, yes, but there are so many things that could cause it," said Stevie. "I mean, lameness can be caused by laminitis, a bruise, a sprain, a strain, a

16

problem with the shoe, a feed problem, bog spavin, bone spavin, thoroughpin, or splints."

"It could be from an injury, disease, or parasite," said Lisa.

"It could be minor, major, or even permanent," Carole added.

"Oh my," said Deborah. "Every time I think I've learned something about horses, I find that there are a million more things to learn."

"A zillion," Lisa corrected her. "Million just covers what there is to learn about the art and science of riding. Zillion is how many things there are to learn about equine health and care."

"And if you add stable management, you're definitely up around a jillion," Stevie said.

"How did you girls manage to learn all these things?" Deborah asked.

"Max, Pine Hollow, Horse Wise," said Lisa.

"Just wanting to know because we love horses," Stevie explained.

"And you, Carole," Deborah asked, "were you born knowing these things?"

"Oh, no," Carole said. "I learned them. I followed the stable boys around at every stable where I rode. Every time they said or did anything, I watched and listened. Sometimes they got a little tired of me, but my father was an officer so they couldn't ignore me—at least, not at the Marine Corps base stables! But any kid who loves horses will find a way to learn these things."

"But don't worry about your baby learning them. As soon as he can crawl, we'll take charge of teaching him everything there is to know about horses," Stevie said.

A worried look crossed Deborah's face. "You mean you think my baby will be as horse-crazy as you girls are?"

"Of course he will be!" said Carole.

Stevie nodded in agreement. "That little one is going to be next in a long line of horse lovers. It's inevitable," she promised Deborah. "I mean, Max did tell you about his father, didn't he?"

"And his grandfather?" Lisa added.

Deborah nodded. "Sure," she said. "I know that the man I married is Maximilian Regnery the Third and that his grandfather founded Pine Hollow and passed it on to his son, who passed it on to my Max. I know that horses are in his blood and probably will be in our baby's, too. But how am I going to be a mother to a kid who loves something I hardly know anything about?"

Stevie laughed at Deborah's concern. "I wish I'd been as lucky as your baby will be!" she said. "Your baby will be with horses from the very first day of his life! I had to wait until I was about in fourth grade!"

"Much later for me," said Lisa.

"I was in kindergarten or something like that," Carole said. "But Stevie's right. Your baby only has to wait a month now—until he's born, I mean."

A strange look crossed Deborah's face. "I don't think so," she said.

"Oh, yes," Lisa assured her. "I'm positive that Max will have his son up and out in the barn within days of the time he's born. It's never too early to start that kind of training."

Deborah winced. "I don't think it'll be a month," she said.

"Well, maybe he'll wait until the baby is like a week or two," Stevie said.

Deborah cringed. "I mean I don't think we'll have to wait as long as a month," she said.

"No, more like a couple of weeks," Stevie said, repeating herself and wondering why Deborah hadn't understood her.

"But don't worry, Deborah," Lisa said calmly. "I know that the last month of pregnancy goes very

19

fast. I heard my mother talking with a friend of hers about it. It'll be over before you know it."

"No," said Deborah. "It'll be over before *you* know it. I mean, it *is* over!"

All three girls pulled their horses to a halt and looked at Deborah. As they watched, the pained look on her face cleared. She glanced at her watch. "Now, let's see how long it is until the next one," she said.

"Next what?" Carole asked suspiciously.

"Contraction," Deborah answered. "And I think it'll probably be a good idea if we head back to Pine Hollow now. Not that I haven't enjoyed this ride . . ."

"Y-You mean—" Stevie stammered.

"Yup," said Deborah.

"It's *now?*" Lisa asked.

"That's right," Deborah confirmed.

"Really?" asked Carole.

"Really," Deborah said. "Now is the time. Today's the day. I am about to turn myself into a mother, Max into a father, and Mrs. Reg into a grandmother. . . . And you three?"

"Into baby-sitters!" Lisa declared.

"Let's go!" Stevie shrieked. With that, she turned Belle around and kicked her firmly into a canter.

"Whoa there!" Deborah called. Stevie drew on the reins and Belle came to a sudden halt.

"Here? *Now?*" Stevie asked frantically.

"No, not here and now," said Deborah. "We've got a good long time, and racing back to Pine Hollow won't help anything. We can walk at a leisurely pace, and when we get back, we'll call my doctor and let him know that the process has begun."

"And Max. Should we call Max?" Lisa suggested.

"Not yet," said Deborah. "This labor is likely to take about twenty hours. There's no reason why Max should be rushed back here. He'll be here for most of it—and for the most important part, anyway. For now, you girls can take care of me, can't you?"

"Of course we can," Stevie said. "We're The Saddle Club. We can accomplish anything when we work together!"

"Isn't that what Max said he was afraid of?" Deborah asked, teasing.

The girls couldn't help themselves. They burst into laughter as they began a gentle walk back to Pine Hollow.

3

ALTHOUGH DEBORAH INSISTED she didn't need any help, The Saddle Club insisted she would get it. Stevie and Carole took the horses to the stable. Lisa tucked her arm under Deborah's and walked with her into the house. Deborah called her doctor.

"Uh-huh, right. . . . Definitely. . . . No, he's not here. . . . I'm fine. . . . No problem. . . . Yes, somebody's here with me. . . . Fifteen minutes. . . . Sure, right," she said. Lisa listened carefully, trying to figure out what the doctor was saying so she'd know what to do when the ambulance got there.

22

Deborah hung up the phone and asked Lisa if she'd like to play some Scrabble.

"Until the ambulance gets here?" Lisa asked.

"No," Deborah said, shaking her head and smiling. "There's no ambulance coming. The doctor isn't rushing over. There's nothing to hurry about because it's going to be a good long time before anything needs to be rushed at all—if ever. My instructions are to stay calm, walk around if I feel like it, and don't eat anything. I'm supposed to call and report progress every once in a while, and he definitely wants to hear from me when my contractions are five minutes apart. That's not likely to be for another twelve hours or so. We've got plenty of time to play Scrabble, read a book, tell stories. See, there isn't even any need to call Max because he'll be back long before then. If we call him now, he'll worry, and that won't do me or the baby any good. And he'll also miss the meeting. He's leading a workshop on handling obstreperous kids, and I know the rest of the Pony Club directors would hate to miss that."

"There aren't any obstreperous kids in Horse Wise!" Lisa said.

"Well, then I guess Max knows what he's talking about," Deborah said with a smile.

23

Lisa laughed. She decided that if Deborah could make jokes, there probably wasn't any need for an ambulance. She didn't know an awful lot about women having babies, but she did know about veterinary care of horses, and one of the things that an owner always had to be sensitive to was a change in basic character. If a normally sweet horse became moody and naughty, it could be a sign of a medical problem. As long as Deborah could joke like usual, that seemed to Lisa to be a sign of good health.

"Okay, so where's the Scrabble set?" she asked.

Lisa was behind by twenty-three points by the time Stevie and Carole came from the stable. Deborah agreed to let the three girls work together. In no time, they'd put *hacking* with the *k* on a Triple Letter and *quirt* on a Double Word with the *q* on a Double Letter. It wasn't easy, either, because Deborah didn't know what either word meant. Lisa explained patiently that *hacking* was what they had been doing when they went on their ride in the woods, and Carole gave an intricate explanation of the braided leather quirts that Western riders used instead of whips or crops. Deborah was a good sport until Stevie came up with a way to use all seven letters for a fifty-point bonus with *jodhpurs*.

"Help! I give up!" Deborah declared, looking at

her measly 125 points versus The Saddle Club's 342. "Maybe you weren't kidding when you said you could do anything when you worked together."

"Well, as long as it has to do with horses," said Lisa, looking proudly at the Scrabble board with all their other joint works, including *mare*, *foal*, and *stall*. Plus, they'd built *colt* on the *c* in *hacking*.

"Maybe you three should try to do something really hard now," said Deborah.

"Like what?" Stevie asked, eager for the challenge.

"Anything that doesn't have anything to do with horses," Deborah said.

"Why would we want to do that?" Carole asked.

"Oh, I don't know," said Deborah. "Sometimes you have to do things just to prove to yourself that you can. I mean, there was a time in each of your lives when you didn't ride horses, talk horses, breathe horses, and live horses, wasn't there?"

"Not so long ago," Lisa said, remembering that she'd only begun to ride recently.

"Well, there was life before you rode horses," said Deborah. "I mean, you did things, learned things, played things—oh, dear . . ." A pained look crossed her face and she glanced at her watch.

"It wasn't that bad," said Stevie.

25

"It's a contraction," Deborah explained. The girls watched her. In a few seconds, the uncomfortable look left her face. "There, it's over." She looked at her watch again. "It was fifteen minutes since the last one, so that's the same as it was."

"Is that good?" Lisa asked.

"It's normal," said Deborah. "It'll take a long time for that to change. There's still no hurry at all. So, now, where were we?"

"Would you like us to read to you?" Lisa suggested. "I've got my copy of *Black Beauty* in my backpack."

"Thanks, but I don't think so," Deborah said.

"I brought *National Velvet*," Carole offered.

"I'm rereading *Misty of Chincoteague*," Stevie said. "I don't have it with me, but it's in my house and I could run and get it if you'd like."

Deborah burst into laughter. "You three are absolutely incorrigible!" she declared.

"What does she mean?" Carole asked.

"Beats me," Stevie said. "Seems to me we're all reading great books."

"Are you just annoyed because we beat you at Scrabble?" Lisa asked.

Of course the girls all knew exactly what Deborah was talking about. They were teasing her back.

26

"No. What were we talking about when my contraction started?" Deborah asked.

"Not we—you," Carole said. "You were talking about the time before we rode horses."

"That's it, then," said Deborah. "I don't want you to beat me at Scrabble with horse words. I don't want you to read to me from your horse books. I want each of you to tell me a real-life story that really happened to you."

"Great," said Stevie. "There was the time Belle and I—"

"No. I want to hear stories that don't have anything to do with horses."

"What for?" Carole asked.

"Well, my baby is going to be surrounded by horses and horse talk all of his life. Horses are fun, but they aren't everything. I'd like to know that somehow, something other than horses was ever important to the three of you. I've got to admit that I find the idea that I'm about to be a mother even scarier than the idea that I'm about to have a baby. So, I need some help. I know I can always get help from you about horses. Give me some help about mothering."

The girls looked at one another.

"No horses?" Carole asked.

27

"Not a one," Deborah said.

There was a long silence.

"How about a cup of tea?" Lisa asked.

"Sure," Deborah agreed. "It'll probably help inspire your storytelling. I'll let you fix the tea. The doctor said I shouldn't eat anything, so just bring me some ice chips to munch on. I'll wait here for you." She put her feet up on a chair, leaned back, and closed her eyes.

The girls hurried out of the living room into the kitchen, where they had a quick conference.

"Is she okay?" Stevie asked.

"No horses?" Carole echoed, still stunned by the idea that she might actually have something to say that didn't have to do with her favorite subject. When she wrote a history paper, it was about the cavalry in the Civil War. In English, she'd only been happy when they'd read "Charge of the Light Brigade." Horses were everywhere in Carole's life. She always assumed that that was fine with everyone around her. Now Deborah wanted something else.

As usual, Lisa was the voice of reason. "Come on, girls," she said. "Deborah is acting a little odd because she's about to have a baby. It's normal. I heard her talk to her doctor. She's supposed to take it easy and keep track of her contractions. If her

28

idea of taking it easy is having a day off from horse talk, well, it doesn't seem like such a big deal to me. We can do this for her."

Lisa took cups and tea bags out of the cabinet while Stevie filled the kettle and Carole found sugar and milk.

"Max would want us to do it," Stevie agreed. She checked to see if the saucers she'd found matched the cups Lisa had gotten out. The cups were green and the saucers were blue. That was close enough. Stevie put them on the tray.

"Max couldn't do it any better than we can," said Carole, pouring milk into a pitcher that had ponies playing all around it.

"Oh, yes, he could," said Stevie. "I once heard him talk about a restaurant he went to."

"I heard that, too. And the restaurant was owned by one of the riders at the stable," said Carole. "So it doesn't count."

Lisa poured boiling water into the teapot, covered it with a tea cozy, and lifted the tray.

"Girls, Max asked us to take care of Deborah while he was gone. If this is how Deborah wants us to take care of her, then we'll do it. After all, we are The Saddle Club, and when we work together, we can accomplish anything. Right?"

29

"As long as it has to do with horses," Stevie said grumpily.

"Well, think of it as doing what we can to help Pine Hollow. After all, this is Max's baby we're talking about—Max the Fourth. One day, this baby will own Pine Hollow and teach kids how to ride. We have to make sure that his birth is as pleasant as possible for his mother. So, if you think about it that way, it *is* about horses."

"Sort of," Stevie agreed.

"I guess so, a little anyway," Carole conceded.

"I'll go first," said Lisa. "Come on."

The girls followed her back into the living room. As soon as they walked in, Deborah's eyes opened expectantly.

"I wish Max were here to hear this!" she teased.

Lisa set the tray down. She handed Deborah a little dish filled with crushed ice. Then she poured tea for her friends. It didn't take anywhere near as much time as she had hoped. In a matter of seconds, Deborah and her friends looked at her curiously. She took a deep breath and began.

LISA'S STORY

I

When I was in fifth grade, Ms. Stevens was the drama teacher at Willow Creek Elementary School, and she decided that we should do a big holiday production. She chose *A Christmas Carol*. All that fall, there was a buzz of excitement in our class. Our homeroom teacher, Ms. Barnard, read us the whole book, and then we read the play. Everybody knows the story, I think. It's all about a mean old miser named Scrooge who has lost sight of what's important in life and just lives for money. He's got plenty of that, but it's really all he has. Ms. Barnard explained that he was so miserable that he didn't even know how miserable he was. Then one Christmas Eve the ghost of his dead business partner comes to his room and tells him that he's going to be visited by three spirits, one of Christmas Past, who shows

31

him how wonderfully happy he was in his early years; one of Christmas Present, who shows him how some poor people are really much happier than he is with all his wealth; and one of Christmas Future, who shows him how bleak his world will be unless he changes his ways. For most of the play, Scrooge is a really despicable man. He doesn't even want to let his employee have a day off for Christmas! The employee is Bob Cratchit, and his son is Tiny Tim—you know, the one who says, "God bless us, every one!"

I wanted to be the Ghost of Christmas Past in the worst way. We only read the book once in class. I must have read it four more times at home, and that was my favorite character. She was wonderful. She got to take Scrooge back to his childhood and through the beautiful Christmasses when there was happiness in his heart. I knew, too, exactly what she should wear. I had a black tutu that I had from my ballet recital of *Swan Lake*. It was perfect for the Ghost of Christmas Past, because she's sort of a delicate child as well as an adult. Ms. Stevens said she was ethereal. That sounded like my ballet dress, even though I didn't know what it meant. All I'd have to do was add something Christmassy, maybe some holly in my hair or something like that, and my dream would come true.

My mother was as excited as I was. In fact, she might have been more excited. You know the way she gets. She even wanted me to take extra acting lessons so I'd get the part I wanted.

"Are you sure this is a story that's going to help me know how to be a good mother?" Deborah asked.

"The best," Lisa said.

"What does ethereal mean?" Stevie asked.

All three girls looked at Deborah.

"Airy and delicate," Deborah said. *"Sort of like a ballet dress."* Lisa smiled proudly and continued her story.

So, anyway, on the day of the tryouts, Ms. Stevens gave everybody a copy of the script and a chance to read as many parts as they wanted. I only wanted one, so I only read for one part. The problem was that I had to try out with somebody else, and that somebody else was, of course, Scrooge. She chose Larry Titus for the job.

"Oh, gross!" said Stevie.

"The worst!" Carole added.

"A creep?" Deborah asked.

"Worse. He's a brat and a bully and a pain in the

33

saddle area," Carole explained. "The only good thing about him is that he moved out of town last year."

"He's the kind of boy who pulls wings off flies," Stevie explained.

"Oh dear, sounds like a perfect Scrooge," said Deborah.

"Well, he was mean enough," said Lisa. She poured some more tea into everybody's cup and then continued her story.

"I am the Ghost of Christmas Past!" I said.

"Give me a break!" said Larry.

Everything he did made me look bad. He confused me and he made me flustered. I completely lost track of where I was in the script, because he wasn't in the script. He just sort of said what came into his mind, and it wasn't ever very nice. Ms. Stevens had to tell him everything to say. He said it all with a snarl.

He was the meanest, crudest, rudest boy in the class, and when he got on the stage, everybody who was watching just sort of cringed.

Ms. Stevens made us wait three days before she announced the cast for the play. I think it was just about the longest three days I ever lived. I will never forget sitting in the assembly hall, waiting for the news. Ms. Stevens had the cast list in her hand.

34

I couldn't imagine what we were all about to hear, but I was sure it was the most important list I had ever heard read. At the very least, I was sure it would mean the end of Larry Titus. There was no way Ms. Stevens would let him have a part when he'd been so awful at tryouts. I kept trying to remember what the smallest part in the play was. I guessed maybe he'd be playing the pawnbroker or something like that. That thought made me feel good all over.

Deborah's brows furrowed suddenly. Her hand went to her belly and she began to massage it gently. She breathed in deeply through her nose and blew it out in a slow stream through her mouth.

Lisa looked at her watch automatically. So did Carole, Stevie, and Deborah. They smiled at one another. It was exactly fifteen minutes since the last contraction. No change. Lisa proceeded with her story.

Naturally, Ms. Stevens gave a talk about how there are no small parts, only small actors.

"I've heard that one," said Stevie. "It didn't make me feel any better when the teacher made me play a tree in the forest in Little Red Riding Hood."

Lisa and Carole laughed. What was funny was the idea that anybody could suppress Stevie's irrepressible personality by turning her into fauna. They were abso-

lutely certain that Stevie had found a way to be the center of attention during the performance.

"But I fooled them," said Stevie, confirming her friends' suspicions. "All during the rehearsal, I kept rocking back and forth, and when my teacher asked me what I thought I was doing, I told her that there was a breeze and my branches were swaying in the wind. When the boy who was playing the wolf got chicken pox, I got his part. Served him right. He wasn't at all scary. I was very scary."

"Let Lisa continue," said Deborah.

Finally, Ms. Stevens read the cast list. Number one was Scrooge. "Larry Titus," she said. I thought she was calling him to tell him to stop doing whatever he was doing. But she actually meant that Larry Titus was going to play Scrooge! I don't think I heard anything at all after that. In fact, I didn't know I'd been made the Ghost of Christmas Past until Cheryl Tripp clapped me on the back and congratulated me.

I just sat and stared. It was as if my worst nightmare and my best dream had come true at the same time. Every second I was onstage, I was going to be with Larry. He didn't like anybody, but he really hated me. He hated me because he was sure that earlier I'd told Ms. Barnard that he hadn't read *The Secret Garden*. That he'd just written his book report from the movie.

I went home that day practically crying. The minute I walked in the door, my mother knew something was wrong.

"Don't tell me. You're one of the Cratchit girls," she said. She didn't like the Cratchit girls. They were just tiny parts and the girls did almost nothing but simper and look pathetically at Tiny Tim or adoringly at their parents.

I didn't want her to worry about this because my mother always worries about things, but I couldn't contain myself. I burst into tears and told her about my part, which made her happy, and about Larry Titus, which made her furious. She said she was going to call Ms. Stevens and make her change the cast. That wouldn't have worked, of course, and it would have made things much, much worse. I told her I'd already made up my mind what I was going to do about the situation.

"I know, I know!" Stevie said, raising her hand as if she were trying to get a teacher's attention.

"Me too," said Carole. Her hand shot up as well.

"I never told you this story, did I?" asked Lisa.

"No, *but we know you,*" said Stevie.

"So, *all right, Miss Know-It-All, what did I do?*" Lisa asked, challenging her.

"*You decided that no matter what Larry Titus did, you would be the best possible Ghost of Christmas Past,*" Stevie said.

"*You do know me, don't you?*" Lisa asked, blushing.

"*That's what friends are for,*" said Deborah.

II

BY THE FIRST rehearsal, I'd memorized all my lines. I'd read the play through so many times that I understood all of it. Remember, I'd taken acting classes the year before. I knew how important it was to understand my character and how she interacted with all the other characters—in this case, just Scrooge, since the two of us are totally invisible to everybody else in the world as we travel back in time. I got a good night's sleep. I wanted to be totally prepared for everything that might happen. As it turned out, I wasn't at all prepared for anything that did happen.

Larry was every bit as much a pain in the rehearsal as he had been in the tryouts. He acted as if he hadn't even read the script through, so everyone thought he didn't know what to say to me. He just kept making up lines as we went along.

"I am the Ghost of Christmas Past," I said. Larry is supposed to ask, "Long past?" and then I say, "No. Your past." Instead, he said "Past what?" He didn't even say it, though, he snarled it.

I looked him straight in the eye. I can tell you there was a gleam in there. He knew perfectly well what he was doing. He was trying to make me goof up, but I decided I wasn't going to let him do it. Every time he messed up a line—and he messed them all up—I figured out a way to get back to the script so he couldn't ruin it for me.

I kept waiting for Ms. Stevens to barge in, and when she didn't, I tried to figure out why. Everyone else in the cast was watching, too. It was like they were waiting for a train wreck. There's a point where I'm taking him back to his school and I ask him if he remembers the path to the building. In the script, he does, but that day, Larry couldn't remember anything.

"Nope," he said.

So, instead of getting flustered, I just told him he should take my hand and I'd show him the way.

Finally, Ms. Stevens said we should take a break.

"Take five"—that's what they say in the theater, like a five-minute break. I just sat down on the bench that was supposed to be Scrooge's bed. Larry ran off with his bratty friends.

Ms. Stevens came over to me and put her hand on my shoulder. "You're doing a great job," she said. "I know Larry can be difficult, but I also know that you'll help him be a great Scrooge. Just hang in there."

Those words meant more to me than I can really tell you. It meant she'd seen everything and knew exactly what was going on. As long as I stuck to my guns, Larry would eventually come around. Or at least that's what Ms. Stevens and I hoped would happen.

What I didn't know was that my mother was watching everything. As soon as I got home that night she told me she'd seen the rehearsal. She had this terribly sad look on her face. I figured she felt sorry for me.

"Lisa, I've heard you practicing your lines," she said very solemnly. "I know you weren't saying the same things onstage that you read out of the script all weekend. You're going to have to work harder to get your lines right or else Ms. Stevens is going to take the part away from you."

40

"Mom—"

"No excuses, dear. I'll test you on them, or your father will if you'd like."

"Mom—"

"I know it was just the first rehearsal, but if you don't do it right from the beginning, it won't be right at the end. I'm sure that's what Ms. Stevens was telling you at the break, wasn't it?"

"It wasn't me!" I said. "It was Larry."

"Now, Lisa, you can't go blaming that boy. He has a difficult part, but he's doing a wonderful job with it. He seems totally into the character, so mean, so rude!"

"Mother!"

"Well, dear, I know you've taken acting lessons. Those classes last year must have done you *some* good or Ms. Stevens wouldn't have given you this part. Still, I could tell that it wasn't working, and if it's not your acting exactly, it must be your approach to the part and to the other characters. Remember, Scrooge is going to have to make a complete change from that horrible character that he is when you first meet him to the delightful and generous man he becomes in the end of the story. It really falls to you to do the bulk of the work. I mean, if he doesn't believe what you show him and

41

begin his transformation with his trip to the Christmasses of his past, well, then he never will. In any event, it's decided, and you'll begin on Tuesday afternoon."

'My mother is like that sometimes. I get this stuff out of left field when I have no idea what's coming. If I've learned anything, it's that she can be the most stubborn woman in the world. Sometimes my dad teases her and says that what she's saying is, "My mind is made up; don't confuse me with the facts." That day was a good example of it. The problem was that Larry was so mean to me that Mom completely believed he was Scrooge. By being good at being bad, he made me look bad—to my mother, of all people.

Anyway, it was decided.

"What was decided?" Stevie interjected.

"Oh, I forgot to tell you?"

"Yes, you did," Carole said.

"Keep on going," said Deborah.

Charm school. Yep, and I'm not kidding about it. My mother had enrolled me in charm school. She'd decided that since I was apparently a total flop as an actress, at least I could learn to be charming, and perhaps that way I could coax a good performance out of myself.

There was a stunned silence. Even Stevie didn't know what to say about this revelation—for a few seconds, anyway. Then she exploded into hysterical giggles.

"I've always known there was something special— uh, charming—about you!" she snorted between waves of laughter.

Lisa tried to ignore the laughter. It wasn't easy, especially when Carole started laughing, too. Even Deborah was chuckling.

"It wasn't a big-deal course or anything." Lisa said. "It was just five classes, given on Tuesday afternoons— like a half course."

"Oh, so you're only half charming!" Stevie hooted.

That remark made Lisa laugh. Carole never stopped. Deborah kept on laughing, but she rubbed her stomach again, too. Everybody looked at the clock. Fifteen minutes. No change. Lisa continued her story.

Mother had already signed me up before I got home, and it became clear that I'd never be able to talk her out of it. I begged, I cried, I promised everything in the world, but, like I said, it was already decided. The only thing I could do was to get her to promise me that in exchange I could do one thing, just one thing, I wanted to do. See, she already had me taking ballet and painting and piano. I like all those things just fine, but I hadn't chosen them any more than I had chosen charm school.

The worst part was that I had to get permission to leave the rehearsals early on Tuesdays. It wasn't a gigantic deal because it was only fifteen minutes and I knew that wasn't going to matter to Ms. Stevens, but I couldn't bring myself to tell her why it was that I needed to leave early.

"Is something wrong, Lisa?" she asked.

"Um, not really," I said.

"I mean, is there something I can help you with?" she asked.

"Just the fifteen minutes on Tuesdays," I said.

She smiled at me. It was one of those kind, sympathetic smiles you get from people who really want to poke into your business.

"The way Robby Kilpatrick leaves early on Fridays?" she asked.

I wanted to drop through the floor. Robby went to a psychiatrist and everybody knew it, but nobody talked about it. He'd been all messed up since his parents' divorce and had started sucking his thumb in math class—not reading group, just math. It turned my stomach to have Ms. Stevens think that I was about to start sucking my thumb in class, but it didn't turn my stomach any more than it would have to have Ms. Stevens know I was being sent to charm school.

"Yes, Ms. Stevens, just like Robby leaves early on Fridays," I said.

I think she believed it, too. After all, she knew my mother.

"Wait a minute. This is supposed to be a story about good mothering," said Deborah.

"Have patience," Lisa assured her. "But in the meantime, you can pick up a pointer or two about stuff not to do, okay?"

"Okay," Deborah said.

III

MISS MARTIN WAS the owner and sole instructor at The Martin Academy. I knew it was going to be trouble before I knew what the name was. Imagine, the very idea of a charm school, but when I heard what she called the place, I figured it was double trouble.

Mother picked me up at school that first Tuesday and handed me a package.

"What's this?" I asked.

"It's your dress," she said.

I guess she figured I had to prove to Miss Martin that I was already charming before I got to the

45

school. We stopped at a gas station and I went into the ladies' room to change. What Mom hadn't counted on was that this was a gas station and the last lady to use the bathroom had obviously had a problem with her car. The whole place was covered with dirty grease and, naturally, it got all over the dress; but it got on my school clothes worse, and there wasn't time to go home, shower, and change, and I'm sure that being late to charm school is an invitation to a black mark by your name. I was covered with smudges of grease when I arrived at my first class.

Miss Martin was unlike anybody I'd ever known before in my life. She was a small woman, thin and frail. It was the middle of the afternoon, and she was wearing a chiffon dress with a stole that she kept playing with. Sometimes she draped it over her head so that she looked like the girl who played the Virgin Mary in the Christmas pageant. At other times she let it flow over her shoulder so that she looked like somebody's fairy godmother. She spoke quietly, in a soft Southern accent.

"Girls," she said when we all sat down. "I am goin' to teach y'awl how to be ladies. Chahmin' ladies. Now I know what y'awl ah thinkin' out they-ah . . ." That's really the way she talked, but

46

I'm not going to try to imitate it anymore, so you're on your own. Just remember that I had to listen to it for two hours that afternoon.

"You're wondering what charm really is, aren't you?" Miss Martin asked.

Naturally, you can imagine that was the last question in my mind. I wasn't exactly on the edge of my seat for the answer.

"Well," Miss Martin said, "it's easy. Charm is five things and five things only, one for each of the letters in the word: C-H-A-R-M." She spelled it in case we didn't know how. "Charm is Cleanliness, Health, Animation, Radiance, and Manners. Once you learn the essence of each of these qualities, you will be ready to go out into the world, demonstrating the finest qualities of the fair sex."

"Argh," said Stevie.

"Five weeks of this," Lisa reminded her.

"I think I'm having another contraction," said Deborah.

"I think I'm going to be sick to my stomach," said Carole.

Lisa continued her story.

Of course, I was just thrilled that my dress and my white socks were all covered with monkey grease from the gas station. It was perfect for lesson one: Cleanliness. Miss Martin decided that I would be the center of attention because there was clearly so much room for improvement. I hated every second of it.

We heard more than I want to tell you about the importance of well-trimmed fingernails—though she didn't consider any of us old enough for colored nail polish. We heard about regular bathing. Every time she mentioned regular bathing, she glanced at me and her right eyebrow twitched upward. At first it hurt my feelings. Then I looked around at my classmates. I didn't know any of them, but I knew one thing about them and they knew it about me. Each of us would rather have been almost anywhere in the world right then but at The Martin Academy, and that suddenly made it all right. In fact, it made it just a little bit fun—maybe too much fun. There was a girl with long red hair who was in trouble. At first I thought she was having a fit. Then I realized that's exactly what it was. She was about to explode into giggles. She clapped her hand across her mouth and made the most horrendous sound.

It startled Miss Martin. But not for long. That lady knew the essence of charm. "Elissa," she said calmly. "Our final lesson will be on manners. I strongly suggest you pay extra attention on that day."

I'm not kidding. She really said that. At that moment, Elissa became my best friend at The Martin Academy. I could hardly wait to see her again next week at Health.

By the end of the two-hour class, I don't think I'd learned a thing I didn't know except a lot of euphemisms Miss Martin liked to use for words she didn't want to say. She didn't say "period," she said "that time of the month." She didn't say "bathroom," she said "water closet" or "loo." The toilet was a "commode." She didn't say "take a shower or bath," she said "bathe." When it came time to discuss underarm odor, she just pointed. She couldn't even say "haircut." She called it a "coiffure."

But one thing I knew for sure was that she was certainly committed to cleanliness. I've never seen anything wrong with it myself. My dress and hands might have been dirty, but my fingernails were clean as can be.

At the end of the first class, I got my first certificate. It said "Most Improved." I still have it, too.

IV

WE HAD ANOTHER rehearsal on Wednesday afternoon—the day after my first charm school class. I certainly wasn't expecting that anything I'd heard from Miss Martin would help me at all, but I was wrong. She'd helped me a lot.

As soon as I entered the part of the stage that was Scrooge's bedroom and looked at Larry, sitting smugly on a bench, holding his script to "help" him remember his lines, I noticed his fingernails. There are clean fingernails and there are dirty fingernails. Larry's were grimy and disgusting. Moreover, he hadn't clipped them properly and they were ragged and uneven. Miss Martin wouldn't like that one bit.

I know it sounds a little silly, but it really did make a difference. I realized then that I had sort of let his obnoxiousness get to me and maybe I hadn't been doing my best. Everybody knows that the Ghost of Christmas Past isn't supposed to go through her scenes in a constant state of annoyance, and that's what I'd been doing. I knew Ms. Stevens didn't blame me, but I sort of blamed myself. When I saw his fingernails, it gave me an edge. Maybe he was obnoxious, but if he cared so little about himself that he couldn't keep his fingernails clean, then I didn't have to worry about him.

I got to the point in the script when I take him back to himself as a lonely child at school. It's sort of a turning point because that's when he first recognizes how isolated he was.

"The school is not quite deserted. A solitary child, neglected by his friends, is left there still," I said.

Larry looked to the blank area of the stage where I pointed. That's his cue to start crying.

Instead, he said, "There's nobody there." One of Larry's friends snickered. I bet he had dirty fingernails, too.

"Ah, but the world can see the lonely child that was to become Ebenezer Scrooge," I said. "He sits forlornly, wondering of his future, his dreams and desires, and having no way to see the bleak future that awaits him."

See, I figured that if Larry wasn't going to do what needed to be done, I'd do it for him. Ms. Stevens caught my eye and gave me a thumbs-up. Larry just glared at me because he hadn't been able to get my goat. All I could think of was how disgusting his fingernails were.

I started wondering what my next class—Health—would bring.

V

AT THE START of the health class, we seemed to take up about where we'd left off.

"Horses sweat, men perspire, ladies glow," said Miss Martin.

"Wait a minute! This isn't supposed to be about horses!" said Deborah. Lisa handed her an ice chip and continued her story.

We had a quick reminder about glowing, and then we went on to a whole new subject: Posture. I know you're not going to believe this because it's so corny, but Miss Martin had us put books on our heads to walk around. Only, it wasn't just any book, it was the book she'd written—and had published privately—that we would each get at the end of the course to remind us of all the things she was teaching us. It was a pretty thin book, so we each had to use two of them. It's tricky to walk around with a book on your head, but downright hard when there are two, since they not only slip on your hair, but they slip on each other.

This wasn't new to me. In acting classes the year before, our teacher had taught us about posture and poise. We had to learn to be a presence onstage. In fact, we were supposed to imagine that there was a piece of space that was ours, that we carried with us wherever we went, and we were to fill that space and use it as we moved. That was a way to hold the attention of an audience.

The result was that I was very good at posture. I stood straight, walked serenely, and held my space, holding everybody's attention as I moved, just the way I'd learned a year before.

"My dear," said Miss Martin. "Surely you don't mean to stand so tall."

I looked down. I looked up. I thought I was probably standing just about as tall as I was, which was about four feet nine inches.

"Why, a girl of your stature who stands so ramrod straight is going to run the risk of being taller than the gentleman who catches her fancy. We wouldn't want that to happen, would we?"

I'd never actually thought much about height and boys before, to tell you the truth. I just figured I'd grow to be the height I was going to grow to and that would be that. I actually liked the idea of being tall. I was tired of having to climb up on chairs to reach things. Miss Martin wasn't in favor of height. Not at all. She thought it was unladylike to be more than about five feet four inches. That's how tall my mother is, and I guessed that's about where I'd end up, but I never worried about it.

Miss Martin implied we should worry about it, especially if we stood tall the way I did. Poor Elissa. Her mother was five feet ten inches tall, and her father was over six feet. At ten years old, she was already over five feet and was doomed to a life of tallness. Miss Martin had a cure for that. She got Elissa to slump a little, pushing her hips forward and then curling her back so her shoulders came forward. It took about an inch off her, but while it might have been charming where Miss Martin came from, I doubt it was really healthy. For one thing, it would make for terrible balance in the saddle— Oops. I mean, if you needed to do something where balance counted, like, say, riding a—uh, bicycle. For another, it can't have been any good for her spine.

Anyway, with Miss Martin's help, I learned not to stand so straight that I looked like a soldier, and Elissa learned to slouch so that her spine was going to go out of joint. That day, Elissa got the Most Improved certificate and I got a little button that said "Fast Learner."

We all had to smile, shake Miss Martin's hand, and curtsy when she gave us our awards. It wasn't easy—the smiling part, I mean.

VI

I WAS ABLE to put lesson number two to work every bit as quickly as number one. We were working on the part of the scene where the young Scrooge breaks up with his fiancée, Belle—

"A beautiful name!" Stevie interrupted. Carole and Lisa giggled. Belle was the name of Stevie's horse. Deborah just glared. Lisa continued.

This is another point in the story where Scrooge gets all upset. He's supposed to beg me to take him home and stop showing him all this painful stuff from his early years.

"Spirit!" he read from his script. "Show me no more!"

"One shadow more!" I say, meaning one more shadow from his past.

Larry got that look in his eyes. I knew he was about to try to throw me off track and say something like, "What part of 'no' didn't you understand?"

He turned to face me, that look in his eyes. My mind flashed. Suddenly I felt as if I had two books on top of my head. I drew myself up to my tallest possible self and there I was, looking down at Larry Titus. It's possible that I might not want to be taller than "uh gentleman who catches muh fay-uncy,"

55

but that definitely didn't include Larry Titus. I was only too happy to be taller than he was. He smirked. I glared.

Then, just like it said in the script, I took his arms, held them to his sides, and led him to the next scene. He didn't kick me. He just went with me. It was a little strange. In fact, while he walked next to me over to the next scene, the wicked twinkle in his eye seemed to melt and he smiled softly.

"Larry! You're supposed to try to cover your face!" Ms. Stevens called out. Larry did cover his face then, but not before I had seen that real, honest, true smile come across it—aimed directly at me!

I'm not proud to say this, but I know I'm with friends and I can trust you and I think it's important to be honest about the past, so I have to say it. Larry Titus got a crush on me. I don't know if it was because I was charming, because I hated him, or because I was suddenly taller than he was, but it's true. From that moment on, he was always totally nice to me.

When the rehearsal was over, I gave him my button that said "Fast Learner." I knew I was in trouble when he clutched it in his hands as if it were a precious prize, looked at it fondly, and then slipped it into his pocket. Big trouble, but I didn't know how big the trouble was.

By the next rehearsal, he'd memorized all of his lines. He said them all perfectly and never missed a cue. That was a relief, but the problem was that there was no meanness to it. He was sweet and kind to me and to everybody else. When he said things like, "If the poor people would rather die than go to poorhouses, they had better do it and decrease the surplus population," he said it as if he really loved poor people and actually loved everybody—and for that matter all the creatures of the earth. He was all sweetness and light, no grump, no grouch, no Scrooge at all. It was a disaster.

There was nothing anybody could do. The Ghost of Jacob Marley yelled at him. Ms. Stevens tutored him. Bob Cratchit begged him. But none of it worked. Larry couldn't be mean and cantankerous anymore. It was as if Scrooge had had a weird personality transplant. Larry Titus spent all his time at every rehearsal smiling at me with these big brown goo-goo eyes of his. It was all I could do to keep from running out of the auditorium in horror.

The following two Tuesdays came and went without any help for me from The Martin Academy. In Animation, Miss Martin wanted us to be bright and witty. She showed us how to draw attention to our-selves in a positive way. It seemed to me that I'd managed to do that very well already—just by being tall—and look where it had gotten me. Even though it wasn't helpful, I loved that animation class because (a) Miss Martin never once men-tioned bathing, and (b) because it was when she showed us what to do with scarves.

I suppose you've always wondered what to do with a scarf. Now I'll tell you: If you're being ani-mated, you fiddle with it. This was apparently what she was doing when she tossed her chiffon scarf over her head or across her front and over her shoulder so that it would flow. The message I got was that if you are in constant motion, people no-tice you. You can't be fidgeting—that just makes people nervous. But an extended arm here or a tilted chin there, plus a "fetching scarf" flung over your shoulder, will surely get you the man of your dreams. I didn't think it would be a good idea to tell her that I'd managed to become the girl-of-his-dreams to the boy-of-my-nightmares by listening in class and then doing the exact opposite.

I, personally, found everything she did with the scarf totally irritating. In fact, it was so irritating to me that I was sure Larry would find it irritating, too. So I borrowed a chiffon scarf of my mother's and tried fiddling with it in the same irritating manner. To tell you the truth, by that time I think I could have been chewing on my hair and Larry would have found it "chahmin'." That's how far gone he was. He seemed bedazzled by the scarf. I didn't bring it again.

The following week was Radiance. That was Miss Martin's code word for makeup. Some of the girls were old enough to wear lipstick, but we all would be eventually, so it was kind of fun to have Miss Martin give us a complete lesson.

She explained that the secret to good makeup was accentuating the positive and eliminating the negative, highlighting the weak and masking the overstated.

I sat next to Elissa at the makeup table. There was a whole array of colors, like a painter's palette, only they were all different shades of flesh tones. Miss Martin had hired a makeup specialist to give us this lesson. I have to tell you, it occurred to me that maybe she thought some of us were such beauty challenges that it would take a real professional to overcome "nature's oversights." That's what she called it. I'm not kidding you. Miss Martin was one of a kind. At least I hope she was—I wouldn't want to meet another of her kind.

Anyway, Elissa and I were sitting in front of the mirror and the makeup lady came over. She smiled at Elissa, but her face sort of froze when she looked at me. I was sure she was saying, "Honey, we've got our work cut out here!"

It took her about forty-five minutes to meet the challenge. In the end, she decided that a little bit of pink lipstick and some blusher was all I needed. I've got to tell you, it made me feel like a failure. She had a lot of fun highlighting Elissa's "fine bone structure." Me, I was a hopeless case.

I wasn't feeling too good when I left that lesson. It didn't help when Miss Martin gave me another Most Improved. Shows you I had no radiance at all.

VII

BUT LESSON FIVE, that's the one I remember the best. Manners. I'd been having manners drilled into me by my mother since I could walk. I'm a polite person. I've always been a polite person. I'm considerate, sensitive, and naturally kind. In case I hadn't noticed that, it all became clear when Miss Martin told me that at the very start of the class. To be honest, she said it to all of us. She said she'd gotten to know us well over the previous four lessons, and she was convinced that that was true of all of us. It occurred to me then, even as an innocent ten-year-old, that she was buttering us up to sign up for her advanced charm class—a ten-week deal—but it wasn't going to work for me. Five weeks of charm were all my mother could possibly force me into. Anyway, as I listened to Miss Martin tell us how wonderful we already were, I could see she was leading up to how much better we'd be.

Since I also already thought I knew most of it, I was prepared for the fact that this week, at least, I wasn't going to get the Most Improved award. Something had to go right for me!

At first, there were few surprises. She taught us to shake hands firmly. "No dead fish!" she exhorted us. We also learned to look people in the eye when we spoke with them or greeted them. I didn't have any problem with that. I'd already learned those things.

She had a place set for each of us at her dining table and showed us which fork to use, how to hold our knives, when to begin eating, et cetera, et cetera, et cetera. All old hat to me, though I must say I'd never seen so many forks and I doubt I ever will. Imagine four forks and five spoons at a meal! I can't eat that much. Oh, that was another thing she said. We were to be proper ladies, and proper ladies never ate too much. Forget everything you ever heard about cleaning your plate. Miss Martin said we were to leave food on the plate.

I tried that on my mother one time when she served spinach. She didn't buy it.

Anyway, after we ate our imaginary meal—don't think that stingy old Miss Martin actually gave us food to eat with all those utensils—she got to the section on being considerate.

We were always to remember that other people had feelings and we should try to put ourselves in their shoes and hear what they were saying. It was never acceptable to hurt somebody's feelings. In fact, she made it an absolute: "A lady never insults anybody." That sounded fair to me. I try not to hurt people's feelings or insult them. Then she said it again, only she finished it in a kind of joking way.

"A lady never insults anybody. Unintentionally."

Everybody laughed. It was kind of funny, but it was really mean, too. It meant that she thought it was all right to be snide, to put people down and hurt them, you just had to be subtle about it. It made me wonder. For one thing, it made me wonder about the collection of Most Improved certificates I was getting from Miss Martin. Were those actually insults? Was she trying to hurt me? That kind of remark makes you wonder, and it made me think about what it really meant to be sensitive to other people. What I'm saying is that Miss Martin taught me a lesson without meaning to teach me a lesson—much stronger than the lesson she'd already given.

I couldn't wait until the end of class. Miss Martin had invited our mothers to come to the tea party she was giving for the graduates. What it actually was, was a sales pitch for her advanced course.

We served the tea, poured carefully, ate cookies neatly—without soiling our white gloves!—shook hands, and curtsied to everybody.

"Oh, barf!" said Stevie.

"I think I feel a pain coming on," said Carole, clutching her stomach as if she were about to vomit.

"I do feel a pain coming on," said Deborah. The girls looked at their watches. Still fifteen minutes apart. They watched while Deborah rubbed her stomach gently and breathed soothingly. "Okay," she said when it was over. "Go on."

I was still upset about what Miss Martin had said about insults and worried about whether she meant anything personal to any of us by it. I was so upset that I spilled some tea on my dress and dropped a cookie. My white gloves got soiled when I tried to pick it up. As if that weren't enough, I put way too much milk in my mother's cup of tea, so it dribbled into the saucer and onto my dress while I was walking over to give it to her. The net result of all this is that when I graduated from The Martin Academy, my dress and my hands were as dirty as they were on my first day when they were smeared with axle grease. I certainly wasn't going to get a Most Improved certificate that day!

When we were finally done with our tea, we each got a kind of diploma from The Martin Academy. I had the feeling that if Miss Martin hadn't already filled out the forms before the class, she might have been tempted to flunk me. But my mother was there and the classes were over. It was time to move on. My diploma simply said that I was a graduate of the academy and fully prepared to go on to the full course that they offered. My mother looked at the thing in surprise and began to say something, but I gave her a look that Miss Martin didn't teach us. So Mom never mentioned the idea of me going on to the full course of charm. In fact, now that I think about it, she's never mentioned The Martin Academy again at all. I think she may have decided that it was a waste of time and money in the first place, but, as you'll find out, she'd be wrong. It wasn't a waste at all.

The day after I graduated from The Martin Academy, fully prepared to be as charming as anybody you'll ever know, was the day we had the dress rehearsal for *A Christmas Carol*. Ms. Stevens loved the idea of me wearing my black tutu. I added a pretty red-and-green cape that they had in the costume room, and I put some holly in my hair. I also wore some pink lipstick and a little bit of blusher, just the way I'd learned in Radiance. I looked good and I knew it. I also knew all my lines and all my cues. I knew where I was supposed to be and what I was supposed to do at all times. I was ready.

I can't say the same for Larry. Oh, he'd learned his lines and he'd finally remembered where he was supposed to be, but he couldn't act worth a darn and that splendid mean quality that had won him the part in the first place was totally gone. He was sweet and gooey from the first. He even sounded apologetic when he told Bob Cratchit that he didn't want him to take Christmas off!

We made it through the rehearsal, but everybody

in the cast, except Larry, was glum as could be. This was going to be a disaster unless somebody did something and did it fast.

I went home that night feeling lower than I had since the day I'd learned I was going to have to go to charm school. Larry Titus was the wild beast who had been tamed by my charms. Our play was ruined and it was all my fault—well, my mother's fault maybe, because she'd been the one to make me go to The Martin Academy.

VIII

I DON'T KNOW what made me think of it. It was probably that awful thing Miss Martin had said about insulting people and how it upset me so much that I'd spilled tea and dropped my cookie. I'd really let her get to me and it had made me behave in ways that I didn't usually behave. I mean, I couldn't believe what a klutz I'd become just because I was upset by what she'd said.

School that day was very long. I don't know if I heard anything at all. I had to learn the whole sevens multiplication table on my own later because I didn't hear any of it that day—but that's another story. Ms. Barnard had to call me three times before I realized it was my turn to read a paragraph. It was a disaster. That didn't bother me, though, because I knew however bad the day was, the night was going to be worse. It was the night of our first performance.

After school, Mom made me take a nap. That was probably a good idea. Then we had dinner and I put on my costume. Usually, just putting on that pretty tutu was enough to lift my spirits. Not so that night. It didn't make me feel any better at all. I was blue as blue could be. Dad drove me over to the school. He said he and Mom would be there for the performance and they'd be sitting in the first row and they just knew they'd be proud of me. There was sort of an awkward silence in the car then, because we both knew that something was wrong. He didn't say anything else until he pulled into the school parking lot. Then he stopped the car and looked at me.

"Is there something you want to talk about?" he asked.

"Nope," I said.

"I know you're worried about something . . ."

"I can't talk about it, Dad," I said. I didn't have the heart to go into what Larry was doing to the play, especially after Dad and Mom had gone to the trouble and expense of making me so charming!

67

"Well, darling, I want you to know that whatever it is that's bothering you, I am very certain you will figure out a way to solve the problem. You are smart, hardworking, clever, kind, and all-around wonderful." Then he held out his arms and gave me a hug. It was better than any Most Improved certificate I ever could have gotten. I knew he meant every word he'd said.

"Thank you, Daddy," I said, and I hopped out of the car.

I know this sounds funny, but it was as if there was some sort of energy transfer in that hug. It was exactly what I needed, and it gave me the inspiration to do what I did.

Everything backstage was all confused. Bob Cratchit had lost his hat. Tiny Tim was complaining that his crutch was too short. The Ghost of Christmas Present had a stomachache, and Jacob Marley swore he couldn't remember any of his lines. Ms. Stevens was running all over the place, trying to help everyone at once. But everyone knew that none of that stuff was going to matter much if Larry was as bad in the performance as he'd been in the rehearsal.

I found Bob Cratchit's hat in the girls' bathroom. Tiny Tim had picked up the wrong crutch. It only took me a minute to find the right one in the box of props. I even got a soda for The Ghost of Christmas Present. It calmed his butterflies in a second.

"You're wonderful, Lisa," Ms. Stevens said. "I don't know what I'd do without you. Now, if only you could find some way to make Larry Titus into a decent Scrooge!"

She blushed the second she said that. She didn't like admitting she'd made a mistake in the first place, and she particularly didn't like to be complaining about one student to another. She apologized and asked me if I could forget she'd said that.

"I'll try," I promised. "But it won't be easy. And besides, it's my fault anyway."

She gave me a hug, too, and told me I'd been doing a wonderful job and she was so proud of me.

So, if everybody was so proud of me, how come I couldn't correct the thing I'd made go wrong? That's when it came to me.

I looked at the clock. It was five minutes until we were due onstage. We'd start right on time. Everything was ready. Everyone was dressed. Everyone had on their makeup. All the props were in place. The stage was set. The only thing there was to do for the next five minutes was to get more nervous.

"*Psst*, Larry, come with me," I whispered. I

69

reached out and took his hand, but of course not where anybody could see it. I would rather have been caught dead than to be seen holding Larry's hand.

It wasn't hard to convince him to come with me. He still had that gooey-eyed look. He'd have followed me right off the edge of a cliff, and that was exactly where I was intending to lead him.

The school auditorium has a back door that goes outside. I took him through that door, hoping no one would notice and no one would follow. I had to be alone with Larry.

His eyes lit up when we got outside. I knew I didn't have much time.

"We just have a minute," I said.

"I know," he answered.

"Look, I had to talk to you before we went on stage. I want you to know that it's going to be all right anyway."

"Sure," he said. But he didn't sound sure, and that was what I needed to hear.

"I just wanted to reassure you," I said.

"About what?" he asked.

"That I'm sure you're going to do a good job. And that I am sure nobody in the audience is even going to notice."

"Notice what?" he asked nervously.

"There's no time left. Just do the best you can under the circumstances."

"What circumstances?" he cried.

"Come on," I said. "We've got to hurry."

Just then, the stage door swung open. It was Ms. Stevens. "Larry? Are you out there? The curtain's about to go up. Hurry!"

I pushed him into the light so that she could see he was there. He didn't have time to ask me any more questions I wasn't going to answer. A second later, he was on stage. A second after that, the curtain went up.

Well, I'm not a mind reader or anything, but when you've been the one to write what's going on in somebody else's mind, it's not really hard to read. That night Larry was a mess. All he could think about was what I'd said. He was worried sick about what I'd told him. He didn't know what people weren't noticing under the circumstances. But it *was* freaking him out. And that made him go back to his bullying behavior. He snapped at Cratchit. He growled at Marley. He was great.

And by the time I got on stage, he was downright scared—just exactly the way he was supposed to be. He turned in a better performance than he'd managed in any of the rehearsals. Backstage, Ms. Stevens was wide-eyed and beaming. I was worried because I was afraid he would still be acting mean when he was with the second and third ghosts or at the end, but it worked just right. Before the second act, I clapped him on the back and told him it was working pretty well. That made him feel a little more relaxed, and when he was a little more relaxed, he was nicer, which was exactly what was supposed to happen to him during the play. By the end of it, he was Mr. Nice-Guy. The audience ate it up. They couldn't stop clapping, and it wasn't just my parents, either.

When it was all over, I tried to get out of the backstage area before Larry got to me, but I didn't manage it. He came running over to me.

"What were you talking about?" he asked.

"When?" I asked, batting my big eyelashes at him just the way Miss Martin had taught us.

"About what people wouldn't notice, probably," he said.

"Why, Larry, I just don't remember," I said. I scratched my head as if I were trying to stimulate my brain. "I wonder whatever could I have been thinking of?" I did the eyelash thing again. Then I dashed out the door to meet my parents. Larry tried to run after me, but he was surrounded by his parents and their friends, who wanted to tell him what a wonderful job he'd done. He couldn't run away from them. I was free!

My parents were great. Daddy gave me another gigantic hug. Mom did, too. She told me she'd known that all I needed was confidence and she thought we could thank Miss Martin for some of that.

I laughed. "Oh, Mom, you don't know how right you are!"

"WAIT A MINUTE," said Deborah. "I'm sure the play was such a success, but you promised that this was going to end up being a story that would give me an example of how to be a good mother. I was waiting for that, and now that we've reached the end, I'm still waiting."

"You didn't get it?" Stevie asked her.

"Are you telling me that if Max and I have a daughter, I'm supposed to send her to some silly lady to teach her to be a wimpy boy-chaser? Or how to be sneaky?"

The three girls laughed.

"No, that's not the point at all," said Stevie. "Although I must say I'm impressed. I didn't know that Lisa had it in her to be that sneaky before she met me. I could learn a thing or two from *her*." She patted Lisa on the back. "Good job," she said. "I'm proud of you, too."

"Back to the subject," said Deborah. "Exactly what is it that I'm supposed to learn from that story?"

Carole took her hand. "Deborah," she said, "you forget that Lisa learned the art of storytelling from Mrs. Reg, your mother-in-law. Don't tell us she never told you a story?"

"Oh, she does it all the time," said Deborah. "When she finishes one of her stories, I often find myself wondering why on earth she told me that particular story, and I always know that if I work at it long enough, I'll get the message. But as I think about this one, I don't know what I've missed."

The girls laughed because that was exactly the way they always felt about Mrs. Reg's stories. They were surprised, however, that Deborah had missed the point of Lisa's story. It was so obvious!

"Easy," said Stevie. "It has to do with the promise that Lisa exacted from her mother in exchange for going to charm school."

Lisa grinned. She knew her friends would figure it out.

"I still don't get it," said Deborah. "You never told us what it was you made your mother let you do."

Lisa just kept smiling.

"She didn't have to tell us," Carole said, laughing. "It's easy. You made your mother let you take riding lessons. Right?"

"Of course!" said Lisa. "What could be a better example of really good mothering than that?"

"Incurable. You girls are incurable!" said Deborah. But she was smiling.

And then she stopped smiling. "Oh dear," she said. "It's another contraction, and it's stronger this time." She massaged her stomach and took a deep breath through her nose, then blew out smoothly through her lips, almost whistling. The girls looked at their watches. It was twelve minutes since the last contraction.

"They're getting closer together," Lisa said. "Should we call the doctor?"

Deborah shook her head as the contraction passed. "No, he said there would be no need to call him again until they were five minutes apart. That's hours and hours away. So, who's next?"

76

She looked at Carole and Stevie. Carole and Stevie looked at one another.

"I guess it's my turn," Stevie said.

"Let the games continue!" Deborah announced as she fluffed a pillow and put it behind her neck.

Stevie took a deep breath and began.

STEVIE'S STORY

I

WELL, THE FIRST thing I should tell you is that my brothers and I have not always gotten along as well as we do today.

Unfortunately, at the moment the words came out of Stevie's mouth, Carole was taking a sip of tea. She couldn't help herself when she heard what Stevie said. She snorted, and an explosion of laughter brought forth a spray of tea. She stopped most of it with her hand, but then had to wipe up the rest of the mess while laughing uncontrollably. Lisa was no help. She was rolling on the floor with laughter.

"Oh dear," said Deborah. "Does this mean that Max and I should only ever have one baby?"

"Yes," said Stevie.

"No," said Carole and Lisa.

Deborah rolled her eyes. Stevie continued her story.

78

Well, the way we got along was different then, because we were littler. Chad was the big brother and he always did everything first. He learned to swim first. He rode a bike first. He lost his teeth first. Everything for him was first. Then came Alex and me. Since we were twins, it seemed like the whole world spent all day every day comparing us. It was "Stevie has lighter hair," or "Alex can climb trees better," or "Stevie is a better reader," or "Alex runs faster, doesn't he?" Every time somebody made an observation about either one of us, it was a comparison, and one of us came out ahead of the other.

In fairness to my parents, I've got to tell you that they didn't do that. They knew better. They'd just tell me how proud they were that I could read so well, or they'd admire how fast Alex could run. They tried really hard—and they still do—but I know that when they admired my reading, Alex would wonder what was wrong with the way he read. I know it because when they admired how quickly Alex ran, I wondered if they'd noticed how fast I could run. To tell you the truth, it was a no-win situation for them.

The thing I had going for me was that I was the girl in the family. That was how I stood out. People would describe us as "the boys and Stevie," and I liked that. My brothers got bunched in, but I got singled out. That made me feel better. Until Michael arrived. First of all, he was cute as a button. That's what people said all the time. I never saw anything particularly cute about buttons, but apparently my parents' friends have been admiring buttons for years, and Michael qualified in that department.

I didn't think he was so cute. For one thing, he couldn't do anything. He just cried and slept. Every once in a while, he'd gurgle, drool, or spit up, and all the adults around would act as if that were the most exciting thing in the world. If I did it, I'd get sent away from the table!

Now, some people might just decide to give up at this point, maybe join up with the ogling adults or at least stop trying to get noticed. Not me. I decided to be the best possible Stevie. By that, naturally, I meant that I was going to be better than my brothers at everything no matter what.

It was easy being better than Michael. All I had to do was burp louder. Anybody could do that, so I set my sights on Chad and Alex. If Alex climbed to the sixth set of branches in the tree in front of our house, I climbed to the seventh. If Chad swam two laps of our pool, I swam three. Of course, I nearly drowned doing it because I wasn't nearly as good a swimmer as he was, but I did it and Dad said he only lost ten years of his life dragging me out of the water. Seemed to me like a fair trade-off.

Chad and Alex and I played together a lot because we had to. I mean, we were in the same house and we were too young then to have friends over *all* the time the way we do now, and, besides, Chad hadn't discovered girls yet. We played cops and robbers, cowboys and Indians, pirates and sailors—you name it. The two of them always tried to get me to be the loser. I got to be better at robbing than they were at policing. I figured out how the pirates could clear the seas of all the galleons of gold. In short, I was good. But they ganged up on me. One robber could defeat one cop, but with two against one, I was a sure loser.

I don't like losing. I never have.

Lisa and Carole exchanged glances. They didn't have to say anything. They both knew they'd heard the understatement of the year. They didn't have to explain it to Deborah, either, since she was politely smirking into her napkin. Without a doubt, Stevie was the most competitive person any of them had ever known.

"Oh, go ahead and laugh at me," Stevie said to them. "Hating to lose has made me work harder and do *better than I would have thought I could at a lot of things. But that's another story."*

It wasn't easy being a younger and a twin sister to two boys. Chad was better at soccer, touch football, even kick the can. Alex was good at all of these things, and better than I was. I was just a girl. I began to wish that I'd been born a boy so that I could be as "good" as they were. I wanted to be as good as someone.

And then there was Michael. He'd stopped being compared to buttons by this time. He's three years younger than Alex and me, so I guess he was about five and I was eight when this all happened. It was like I'd never much noticed him before, and then suddenly he could play soccer and kick the can with us. He was having a ball at it, and I was beginning to have fun, too, because suddenly there was someone I was always better than. I could always beat him in a race, run faster, jump higher, play better. I found it very satisfying. The fact that my skills—to say nothing of my attitude—often left my little brother bathed in his own tears didn't bother me in the least. I was number one compared to somebody, and that was all that mattered to me.

My parents had a different point of view on the subject. I suppose my mother was a little tired of constantly having to comfort Michael, and my dad wasn't too pleased with having to explain to me, every single day, that Michael was younger and it was my responsibility to look after him, not just to beat him. It wasn't a lesson that sank in very well. To my parents' credit, they tried not to yell at me about what I was doing. They actually did understand how tough it was for me to be the one girl in a crowd of boys. They thought that if they yelled at me, I'd just start hating Michael. Of course, they were completely wrong there. I couldn't hate him. He was the only one around I could always beat. He meant a lot to me!

"Deborah, I'm trying to give you some pointers here on mothering. It's really important to understand what's going on in your kid's mind. You've probably heard a lot about things like grounding and removing privileges and time-outs. Forget that stuff. Keep in mind words like treat *and* extra television time *and* raise in your allowance, *okay?" Stevie said. Then she continued her story.*

Anyway, my parents tried very hard to change the situation. About the only time there was ever total peace in the house was when Mom or Dad was reading to us. We loved to have them read to us. They read anything and everything and we listened

83

to it all. My favorites were the animal stories, like *Charlotte's Web* or the Uncle Remus tales. Alex liked stories about history, like *Johnny Tremain,* and Chad would listen to anything that was science fiction. His all-time favorite was *A Wrinkle in Time.*

When we weren't hearing a good story, that's when trouble broke out. To be perfectly honest—not that I'm ever *not* perfectly honest, mind you—I was actually being something of a bully to Michael. Somewhere along the line, Mom and Dad figured that this probably wasn't very good for Michael or for me. That was when they decided to "Do Something about Stevie."

That's what I heard Mom say. She was talking with her mother on the phone. Now, at that point, I think my mother's idea of Doing Something might have been to send me to reform school. She was pretty fed up with me, so it was my lucky day that Mom was saying that stuff to Granny. Because Granny's idea of Doing Something had nothing to do with reform school. I could only hear one end of the conversation, and if Mom had known I was sitting on the other side of the wall, I wouldn't have heard any of it. But I could tell from what Mom was saying that Granny was on my side.

"Well, of course it's hard for her. . . . The boys

gang up on her, sure. . . . What do you mean, 'make it possible for her to be a girl'? . . . But Mother, she *is* a girl. I only have one daughter. . . . Well, I suppose . . . I suppose I could take some time off. . . . But where? Who? Oh, I have an idea. Maybe you're right. . . ."

It went on from there, but the rest is unimportant because by then my mother had decided and all it took was a few more phone calls. Believe me, I didn't move an inch from where I was sitting. I didn't want to miss anything. I wasn't exactly sure what was coming, but I knew I was going somewhere with my mother, no brothers, not even Dad. Just me and Mom.

It turned out to be more than that, too. Mom had this friend from college who lived in Massachusetts. Her name was Annie Pine. They hadn't seen one another for years, but they talked on the phone a lot and Mom got letters and Christmas cards from her. It seemed that every Christmas card talked mostly about her daughter, Madeleine. Madeleine was just my age, eight. She was pretty and she was smart.

I still remember almost everything my mother said on the phone when she called Mrs. Pine to see if we could come for a visit. No, that's not true. I don't remember much of it, but I do remember her saying, "Stevie's been having a rough time this year. It breaks my heart to see such a precious child have such a difficult period." She called me precious. I wasn't more precious than one of my brothers, or less precious. I was simply precious to her. It made me feel about two feet taller. It wasn't as if my mom never told me she cared about me, but there she was telling someone else how great I was. Sometimes I've thought that maybe we could have skipped the rest of the trip to visit the Pines and just stopped there. But that wasn't what happened, and this is, so I'll get back to it.

Before I knew it, Mom and I were on a plane. I loved the plane ride. I spent a lot of time looking out the window, and I also spent a lot of time telling Mom the things I wanted to do with Madeleine when we got there. I bet that she liked to play kick the can and soccer. I thought it would be fun to have races with someone who wasn't my brother, to climb a tree with somebody who didn't want to get me to sit on the far end of a limb while he wiggled it so much I almost fell off. The Pines lived near a lake. I couldn't wait to go swimming in it and show Madeleine that I could swim under water a whole long way. If she could do things I couldn't, I'd ask her to show me how. Maybe she could do a backwards somersault into the lake. I wanted to learn how to do that. We could play Monopoly and Clue—if they had those games. We could paint mud pictures on wood. We could build a miniature fort out of twigs. I even wrote down a list of all the things I could do during the visit. My mother helped me spell *somersault*. The whole flight was just wonderful.

It was great when we arrived, too. Mrs. Pine and Madeleine were both there. Mrs. Pine had a big grin on her face and gave Mom a gigantic hug—me, too. Madeleine shook hands with me. I guess that was polite, but it seemed a little strange. I never had a kid my own age shake hands with me, but I just figured maybe she was a little bit shy and didn't know how to smile very well. I was sure this would change, and I was right.

We all got into the car to drive back to the Pines' house. Mom sat in the front seat with Mrs. Pine. The two of them were talking a mile a minute about all the people they remembered from college and what had happened to them. Madeleine and I didn't know most of the people they were talking about, so it wasn't a very interesting conversation, but it was more interesting than what we said to one another, which was almost nothing.

I thought about the list of activities I'd made on the plane, and suddenly it didn't seem as if we'd play any of the games I wanted to play. Finally Madeleine said something.

"Did you have a good trip on the plane, Stephanie?" she asked me.

Now, you know me and you know that nobody in the world ever called me Stephanie. I wasn't even sure who she was talking to.

"Oh, right, yeah, it was a good trip," I said. "Everybody always calls me Stevie," I said. "That's short for Stephanie—kind of a nickname. I bet you have a nickname. Do your friends call you Maddie?"

There was this big long silence. I think our mothers even stopped talking. Just as I'd never seen someone my age shake hands with a friend, I'd never seen someone my age who could look down her nose at you—I didn't know Veronica diAngelo then—and Madeleine took in a deep breath of air.

"Nobody," she said, "ever called me Maddie, and I trust that nobody ever will. My name is Madeleine."

I gulped. She pronounced it so that the *-leine* part rhymed with her last name. No sloppy pronunciation that might result in a sort of "Mad-uh-lin." I'd already learned the first thing that Madeleine Pine was going to teach me. It wasn't a lesson I was likely to forget—or forgive.

II

MADELEINE'S ROOM WAS bright and sunny. It was all decorated in pink, with dolls on all the shelves. Where there weren't dolls, there were doll things—houses, teacups, all that stuff. Most of it was new to me. I'd been brought up with soccer balls, baseball bats, and tennis rackets. I didn't think I'd missed much with only a few dolls, but I've got to say that Madeleine's collection was impressive.

There was one that was particularly nice. She had shiny brown hair and the prettiest pink dress I had ever seen. I dropped my suitcase and walked right over to the shelf where she was kept. I reached up to take the doll down so I could look at it more closely.

"Oh, please!" said Madeleine. "That's a valuable doll that my father bought me in Europe when he was on a business trip. Her name is Elena. She's not for playing. She's for show. I guess I should keep her in a locked glass cabinet so people who don't know any better won't try to touch her."

I blushed. I felt terrible that I was going to touch something that belonged in a glass cabinet.

"I'm sorry," I said. "I didn't know."

"That's all right," said Madeleine. For some reason, I felt better when she told me it was all right. I guess I'd had this idea that what I was going to do was awful and now I was forgiven. Some people really confuse you sometimes, and Madeleine was one of them. She went on to be more confusing.

"I guess you should sleep in that bed," she said, pointing to one of the twin beds in her room. "I was going to have my best friend, Maggie, sleep over tonight, but since you're here . . ."

She really said that, and she said it that way, like maybe I should just disappear so that somebody she actually liked could stay over. All the nice thoughts I'd had on the plane were disappearing fast, but they weren't totally gone. I still wanted this to be a special trip and a special visit. Maybe there was a way.

"Look, why don't we get a sleeping bag," I said. "One of us could sleep on the floor."

"You mean you'd be willing to do that?" Madeleine asked.

"Sure," I said. Only later did I wonder how a suggestion that "one of us" could have gotten turned into "you" by Madeleine. At the time, the only thing I noticed was that I'd made Madeleine smile at me. It was the first smile she'd made since I arrived.

"Stevie!" Deborah said. "This story is supposed to inspire me to be a great mother! All you've told me about is awful children . . . uh, you included. How am I supposed to learn anything from this?"

"Just wait," Stevie said. "I'll get to the good part pretty soon. And besides, remember that my mother had no way of knowing how awful Madeleine was. She really, truly, was trying to do something nice for her 'precious' daughter, okay?"

"Okay," Deborah said. But for a second she didn't look okay. The girls knew by now what was happening. She was having another contraction. Carole stood behind her and massaged her shoulders to help her relax. Lisa held her hand. Stevie looked at her watch. Twelve minutes.

"No change," Stevie said. "Still twelve minutes."

"Shouldn't you call your doctor again to report progress?" Lisa suggested, reminding Deborah that her doctor had wanted her to call.

"Oh, sure," Deborah said. She picked up the phone

and dialed. It turned out that her doctor wasn't there. The answering service told her that he'd left the office for an emergency in Cross County. He wouldn't be available for several hours anyway. They could page him, though. Deborah said that wasn't necessary. She was just reporting that everything was going the way they expected. If the doctor called in, they could let him know that.

"I'll call again later," she said. She hung up the phone and turned to Stevie. "Okay, so what happened next?" she asked.

Well, Maggie arrived then. I thought I'd like Maggie because she had a nickname. She wasn't called Marguerite or anything fancy, just a nice, normal Maggie. She was, too. Normal, I mean, at least compared to Madeleine, but she wasn't all that normal.

"What should we do?" Maggie asked.

I thought about my list of fun things I wanted to do, and I held out this hope that a nice game of tag or kick the can might warm things up between me and Madeleine. She wasn't interested in those games. Maggie just sort of stared at me.

"How about climbing some of the trees?" I asked. The Pines' house was surrounded by woods. There had to be some good climbing trees out there.

"Oh, I don't think so," said Madeleine.

"How about a rock, then? Can we climb some rocks?"

"And get rips in our shorts?" Maggie asked.

I had been ready to suggest a rousing game of cops and robbers, but I could tell that wouldn't succeed any more than anything else I'd suggested. I was about to suggest a game of hide and seek, but I could see myself hiding and nobody seeking. I'm not a fool. It was time to let them make a suggestion.

"How about a tea party?" Maggie said. "We can take our dolls along, the way we usually do."

A tea party, with dolls. I'd never done anything like that. I couldn't imagine having a tea party with my brothers, with or without dolls. Tea parties with dolls was something little girls did. I was a little girl and I'd never done that. Maybe I'd been missing out on something all those years. It was about time I tried something new.

"Okay," I said. "What do we do first?"

It turned out that what we did first was to get Mrs. Pine to do all the work. It was more like a picnic than a tea party. She made a whole little lunch box filled with treats, plus a thermos of tea for us. There were little sandwiches and little cookies. We had small teacups for us and tiny ones for the dolls. Madeleine carried the dolls. Maggie carried the lunch box. I got to carry the blanket.

My mother watched us pack up. She was beaming with pride at her precious tomboy daughter going on such a girlish excursion with Madeleine and Maggie. I was pleased that she was so proud, even though I couldn't imagine why anyone would want a tiny little cucumber sandwich when there was peanut butter and honey to be had. Still, it was a new experience, and I was game to try it.

The Pines' house was really nice and it was in a great place. They were down the street from a beautiful little lake that had a beach. We walked past the lake. I thought it would be nice to have our picnic on the beach, maybe go swimming afterward.

"Oh, maybe," said Madeleine, but I could tell that *maybe* meant "never."

"I can't," said Maggie. "I hate it when I get water in my ears."

I'm telling you, that's what she said—like she'd never heard of hopping up and down on one foot, tilting her head to get the water out of her ears. So much for my bright idea of learning how to do a backwards somersault!

It was like the two of them were two pieces of the same pie. If Madeleine didn't want to go swimming, Maggie came up with the excuse—lame as it was. If I hadn't been feeling left out before, I really started feeling left out then. It was as if they'd joined forces to make me feel bad. I would have felt totally bad if I hadn't had a nice thought at that moment. I decided that Madeleine's name wasn't Mad-uh-line Pine, it was Mad-uh-lane Pain, and I decided to call her Mad-uh-lane for the rest of my visit.

We kept on walking past the beach, and then there, next to the lake, was a really wonderful house. It was old, covered with shingles, and the windows were all boarded up.

"What's that?" I asked, wondering why anybody would cover the windows on such a neat, big old house.

"That's supposed to be haunted," said Maggie. "At least that's what some people say, but, of course, there's no such thing as a haunted house."

I looked at it again. It was two stories with a big pointed roof on top. That had to mean it had a cavernous attic. There was gingerbread trim around the edge of the roof. The shutters that remained had little designs cut out of them, trees, hearts, things like that. It actually made me think of the witch's cottage in *Hänsel and Gretel.*

"I don't know about that," said Madeleine.

"About what?" I asked.

"About there being no such thing as a haunted house," said Madeleine. "I've heard stories . . ." Then, if you can believe it, she actually nudged Maggie.

"Oh, right, yeah," said Maggie, suddenly changing her tune to suit her friend. "Lots of stories, like, uh . . ." Maggie couldn't seem to come up with any on the spot. Madeleine supplied one.

"They say that at night, when there's a full moon, you can hear ghosts howling," Madeleine said. "According to the local legend, it belonged to a mean old sea captain who went away to sea and didn't come back for such a long time that his young wife thought he was dead and got remarried. When he came back and found she'd married someone else, he was furious and tried to kill her new husband. There was a gigantic fight and the new husband killed the sea captain. Then he and his wife lived in the house for the rest of their lives. But they had to live with the ghost of the sea captain. He never left them alone, and on the night of the full moon, everyone in town can hear the howling."

I'd been listening to ghost stories all my life, and I can tell you that Chad could have told a story ten times better than that on the spot. There were a million things wrong with it. In the first place, we were nowhere near the sea, and no self-respecting sea captain would have a house so far inland. For another thing, if you figure your house is haunted by the ghost of your first husband who was killed by your second husband, aren't you going to go find somewhere else to live? And then, there are all the legal complications of a murder, like if it had occurred, wouldn't the second husband have been punished?

Well, never mind that it was a dumb story, I knew she'd just made it up to scare me, and although she might have gotten me to go on a tea party with dolls, I wasn't ever going to let her scare me.

"I'm not the least bit afraid of a silly old ghost," I said.

"That shows how much you know," said Madeleine. "You should be afraid."

III

THE TEA PARTY was another learning experience for me. In the first place, the blanket wasn't really large enough for three girls and three dolls. It seemed to be large enough for two girls and three dolls, though, so I mostly ended up sitting on pine needles. Then, when Madeleine dropped her cookie on the ground, she pretended she'd actually been handing it to me, so it was officially my cookie, and I wasn't too thrilled with the idea of eating a dirt-covered cookie.

Even at the worst, I never felt so unwelcome with my brothers as I did with Maggie and Madeleine. They were doing everything in the world but saying I should go away and leave them alone. If I'd been with my brothers, I would have thought nothing of punching or screaming, but this was different. I still wanted to find a way to make it be all right. That was when I told Maggie that Madeleine and I had decided I could sleep in a sleeping bag on the floor if she wanted to stay the night.

That made them both very happy, but it didn't make me feel one bit better.

Finally the picnic ended and we went back home. I don't remember much of what happened for the rest of the day, but I do know that when it was almost time to go to bed, my mother said she had something in her suitcase that I should get, so I should go with her into her room. I had no idea what she was talking about, but what she had for me was the best present in the world. It was her lap. She sat down in a chair and had me come over for a hug and a talk.

"I don't think this is turning out to be the visit you were expecting," she said as she held me tightly.

I couldn't say anything because she was more right than she could possibly know.

"I don't think you and Madeleine really have very much in common, do you?" she asked.

I just shook my head because I was afraid I might cry.

Mom told me that she and Annie were having a wonderful visit and it meant everything in the world to her to have me there with her and she appreciated the fact that I was trying so hard to be friendly with Madeleine. She was very proud of me, and she was pretty sure that things would get better. Somehow I'd figure out how to enjoy my visit, and in any case I could be proud of myself for being such a wonderful girl. She didn't actually say "precious," but I think that's what she meant.

I was proud of her, too. Some mothers might ignore the fact that their friend has an obnoxious daughter. My mother knew it, and she wouldn't call it any other way.

We didn't have a very long visit, but it was an important one. When we were done with our hug, I was ready to face a night with the obnoxious M girls. I was going to manage to keep my mother proud of me, and I was going to manage to help her have a good visit with Annie, no matter what it took.

You can imagine that the sleepover wasn't one tiny bit better than the rest of my visit had been so far. The one thing it had going for it was that Madeleine and Maggie ignored me totally, so I ignored them. While they talked about dolls, clothes, and the girls in their class, I read my book and then went to sleep. I don't know how long they talked. None of it had anything to do with me.

I don't know what woke me up that night. I couldn't see the clock, but I knew it was the middle of the night. Everybody was asleep. All the lights were out. Outside, I could hear night sounds, crickets, frogs on the lake, things like that. I stood up and looked out the window. Somehow, the summer night with its familiar sounds seemed much more friendly than the house. It was a dumb thing to do, I know, but I just had to get out of there before those two woke up and started talking about Sally Malone's orthodonture.

It was a warm night. All the doors were open so that whatever breeze there was could come through the screen doors. I let myself out and went for a midnight walk. I'd only been there less than a day. I didn't know any place to walk except the way we'd gone past the beach and the old house to where we'd had our tea party. Naturally, that was where I walked. It took me longer at night. It was completely dark out, so it was hard to see where I was going. There were streetlights, but they were far apart. After about fifteen minutes, I was in front of the old house. I was just standing there, minding my own business and admiring the house, when there was a bright flash of light, a loud crack of thunder, and all of a sudden it was pouring rain. Nothing gentle about it. It was a torrential downpour. I realized that I was standing in the middle of a dark street, in the middle of the night, in the middle of a rainstorm, wearing my pajamas. Not real bright, huh?

I needed to get under cover, but even at eight years old I knew better than to hide under a tree in a thunderstorm. For one thing, the rain was coming down so hard that a tree wouldn't have done me any good. For another thing, and probably more important, I knew that a tree was a dangerous place to get shelter in a thunderstorm. A tall tree attracts lightning. I didn't really have a choice. I ran to the porch of the old house. Then, like it was an automatic thing, I pushed at the front door. It opened right away. I ran inside without thinking that the house probably belonged to somebody and that that somebody wasn't me. As suddenly as I'd been in the rain, I was now out of it. That was all that mattered.

There was a light switch on the wall. I flicked it and an old chandelier turned on. I don't know why there was electricity in an abandoned house, but there was, and I'm not one to question good fortune. Ghosts or no, rain or no, I hadn't been too thrilled with being in a big old house in the total dark.

I don't know what I was expecting, but what I found was a really nice old house. Sure it was beat up. Some of the wallpaper was torn and stained.

There were posts missing from the banister. There was a broken chair in one corner and a pile of old newspapers by the fireplace. There was dust on everything, and cobwebs, too, but there was still something totally neat about it. When I thought about it later—like years later—I think I decided that what was mostly neat about it was that Madeleine wasn't there. I smiled to myself and sat down on the pile of newspapers.

Although some of the windows had boards crisscrossed over them, I could see around them to the outside. I could see that the rain was still coming down in buckets, and I could see when there was a giant flash of lightning, which was often. I didn't actually have to see that, though, because every time there was lightning, the lights flickered and then there was a gigantic crash of thunder. It was totally eerie and totally cool. A big gust of wind came through, probably from one of the windows that was broken under the crisscrossed boards. There were curtains on the window, though, and they got picked up by the wind, sweeping into the room.

It was a funny thing. As I sat there, in the dim light and the rain, I could almost believe that there was a ghost in the house. It was the kind of place a ghost might actually like to hang out. It certainly was a place I liked to hang out.

Since the lights worked, I wondered if anything else did. I went to the kitchen sink and turned on the faucet. There was a tiny little dribble of very dirty water, but there was a great big groaning sound in the pipes. Overhead, I heard a creaking noise. The wind had to be blowing a door that was swinging on creaky hinges.

It was perfect. The thought crossed my mind that I should go get all my stuff and move into the haunted house until it was time to go home. Mom could have her visit with Annie. Madeleine and Maggie could have their visit without me. And I could be where nobody would ever bother me.

Oh, there might be a few pesky details like food and water and clean blankets to sleep on, but I'd find a way. Of course, I knew I couldn't do that. I didn't care what Madeleine thought, but I actually did care how my mother would feel. I started thinking about how much I wanted Mom to have a good visit and how I wanted to hurt Madeleine as much as she'd hurt me and I was sure there was no way I could do both things. But then there was another squeaking sound in the house—this time it was the cutest little mouse dashing across the floor—and I began to get the idea that I might actually have found a way to have my cake and eat it, too. In other words, a perfect plan was forming in my little warped brain.

I had just a few small details to take care of before I went back to Madeleine's house. There was no time to waste.

IV

YOU'D THINK THAT one doll tea party a week would be enough for anyone, but it seemed that Maggie and Madeleine couldn't get their fill of doll tea parties. I guess it was some sort of tradition with them or, maybe and more likely, they both knew that it bored me and therefore it was definitely their choice activity. I didn't mind. In fact, I'd been counting on it.

Once again, we packed up everything, selected the dolls that Maggie and Madeleine wanted to play with, and waited for Mrs. Pine to make a picnic for us. This time my mom decided to help, and the next thing I knew one of the sets of finger sandwiches was none other than peanut butter and honey. She was being just wonderful.

By this time, Mrs. Pine had figured out that

things weren't exactly going my way, and I think she was a little embarrassed about the way her daughter and Maggie were behaving toward me.

"Perhaps you'd like to have your guest choose where you go on your picnic today," she said to Madeleine.

"Okay," Madeleine agreed. "Maggie, where would you like to go?"

I mean, she was really that obvious!

"Now, Madeleine," said Mrs. Pine. "Maggie can choose anytime. Why don't you let Stevie choose?"

"But Stevie doesn't know where anything is around here," said Madeleine.

I wasn't going to let the opportunity pass me by. "Well, maybe I don't know where I do want to go, but I certainly know where I *don't* want to go," I said.

"Where?" Madeleine asked, as if she really meant it.

"Anyplace but that haunted house. It's scary!" I said. "I don't ever want to go near there again. In fact, if we could go someplace that doesn't even pass it, that would be fine by me!"

Maggie and Madeleine looked at one another. I'd seen that look before. I'd seen Chad and Alex look at one another like that dozens of times. It always meant trouble for me.

"I'd like to go back to the place where we had our tea yesterday," said Maggie.

"Okay," Madeleine agreed.

"But not past the haunted house," I said.

"There's no other way," said Maggie and Madeleine, practically at the same time.

"Well, then I'm walking on the other side of the street," I said.

Madeleine smiled. Maggie smirked.

We'd hardly gotten out of the house before the teasing began.

"Stevie believes in ghosts!" said Madeleine.

"Whooo-ooooo!" said Maggie. Can you imagine anybody making such a stupid noise, like that was going to frighten me?

Then Madeleine started talking as if she had come directly from Transylvania: "Com eento dee haunted house! Meet dee spirits that invade it ah-vry single night!"

"Whooo-ooooo!" said Maggie again. She wasn't long on imagination.

"Oh, come on," I begged. "Don't make fun of me! I wouldn't be frightened if you hadn't told me about the old sea captain. I was looking at the house yesterday and I was just about sure I could see him through one of the windows!"

"Whooo-ooooo!" said Maggie.

"Oh, come on, let's just have our tea party!" said Madeleine.

So we headed back to the spot in the woods. I was careful to walk at the very far edge of the far side of the road when we passed the haunted house. In fact, I ran as we passed it.

Madeleine stopped when we were just past the house. "Stevie, are you telling me you're really afraid of that house?"

"I guess so," I said. "I don't usually believe in those things, like I told you yesterday. But there's something about that place that gives me the creeps. One hundred percent!"

"Really?" Maggie asked. "You mean that you'd be afraid to go in there?"

"One hundred percent!" I said.

"Yesterday you said you didn't believe in ghosts and you weren't afraid."

"Well, that was before you told me that scary story," I said. "Now I'd hate more than anything in the world to go into that house."

"I dare you," said Madeleine.

I stopped in my tracks and just stared at her.

"Double dare!" said Maggie.

"No, don't make me do it!" I said. I was so excited I'm sure I managed to make my face turn white.

"Only fraidy-cats won't go on a dare!" said Madeleine.

"Whooo-ooooo!" said Maggie.

"I'm not a fraidy-cat!" I said, but I tried as hard as I could to look like one.

"Well, you are, too, if you won't even touch the doorknob."

"Doorknob?" I asked. "Just touch it?"

"Just touch it," Maggie said.

"You'll come with me?"

"That would show how brave we are, not how brave you are," said Madeleine. "We'll watch from here."

"I don't know," I said.

"What's the big deal?" asked Madeleine. "The ghost is only on the inside. The doorknob is on the outside!"

"Well, if I don't have to go in . . ."

"Triple dare!" said Maggie. That sealed it.

"I'll show you!" I said.

"I'm sure you will," smirked Madeleine. She was

totally pleased with herself, and so was Maggie. They'd figured that touching the doorknob would be enough to melt me into a shivering mass of nerves, which, as we know perfectly well, is exactly what they were after.

I ran. I don't think I've ever run so fast in my entire life. I had to cross the road, cross the lawn, cross the porch, and get to the door. I grabbed for the doorknob, twisted it, and, just as it had the night before, the door slid open easily. I screamed loudly while I slipped into the darkness of the house and let the door slam behind me.

In a second, I got to the front window and peered through a crack in the boards. There, on the other side of the street, were Madeleine and Maggie, totally engrossed in a fit of giggles. That, I sincerely hoped, would be the last laugh they had for some time.

They looked at one another. They looked at the house. They waited. They peered at the door. Maggie glanced at the windows. Madeleine shaded her eyes to see the house more clearly. There was nothing to see, nothing to hear. Nothing was happening. There was no sign of a ghost and there was no sign of me.

Madeleine shrugged. Maggie put her hands on her hips. They waited.

Finally they'd had enough. They couldn't leave without me. How would they explain it to our mothers, especially since I'd made that scene about the haunted house? They had no choice but to come after me. They put down the tea party stuff and walked across the street and the porch to the door. They were good and angry with me. I heard their steps on the front porch. I watched them open the door, slowly. Madeleine came in first, followed by Maggie. They looked around. The door slammed behind them, making them each jump again. I loved it—every minute of it.

Then there was a totally startling sound. It was a howling cackle coming from the second floor of the house. Madeleine jumped. Maggie's jaw dropped. I screamed.

"Stevie!" Madeleine howled.

Maggie grabbed her. Madeleine grabbed the doorknob. It fell off in her hand. The door was locked. They were trapped.

The fact that each of them knew, really knew in their heart of hearts, that there was no such thing as a haunted house, that Madeleine had made up the dumb ghost story about the sea captain, and that this was all supposed to be a trick on me didn't change the fact that they were scared. They were so scared they could hardly talk.

"W-W-W-W- . . ." was all Maggie could manage. This from a girl whose only word earlier had been *whooo-ooooo!* I loved it.

"Where is she?" Madeleine said.

The horrendous cackle erupted from the second floor again.

"That's her! I'm gonna get her and I'm gonna brain her!" said the previously refined Madeleine.

I screamed. From the basement. They couldn't fail to notice that the cackles and the scream were from different ends of the house.

"We have to find her," said Madeleine. Maggie would have disagreed if she could have talked, but she was too frightened now to make any sound at all. And although the second-to-last thing in the world she wanted to do was to take one step farther into the house, the last thing she wanted to do was to be separated from Madeleine. She clutched her arm tightly. Together, they stepped forward. They walked to the basement steps.

A ghastly gust of wind penetrated the room, raising all the long white curtains at the same time.

Maggie's mouth opened to form a scream, but nothing came out.

"Come on!" Madeleine demanded.

There was a thump from upstairs, then a muffled dragging sound: *thump-drag, thump-drag, thump-drag,* across the floor above. They glanced at the ceiling, following the sound. It might have been the sound of a lame man. Maybe a one-legged sea captain's ghost?

"Stevie!" Madeleine called out loudly. "Stop that!"

From the basement came my feeble voice, now too weak to scream.

"Helllllp!" I cried, gurgling as if I were drowning in the briny sea.

"Where is she?" Maggie asked, looking first at the ceiling, then at the basement door.

The kitchen door slammed and the water pipes screeched in protest. In the attic, an old ceiling fan sparked to life, slapping noisily at scattered air-borne papers on each turn. And if that weren't enough, a bat flew across the living room, squeaking loudly.

Madeleine screamed and clutched Maggie. The two of them stood frozen in fear, holding one another tightly.

Above them, the thump-drag sound continued slowly and relentlessly toward the rear of the house.

Madeleine took a deep breath. "I'm going to kill her," she said. "Come on."

The two of them headed for the stairs. Slowly, step by step, they came up to the second floor. They were greeted at the top of the steps by a weak flicker of light. Maggie sighed and nearly collapsed.

"It's just a mirror," said Madeleine, dragging her friend to the top of the stairs. To one side of the mirror was a window shade, flapping wildly in the wind caused by a fan next to it.

There was no lame sea captain limping across the floor.

Thump-drag, thump-drag. It was now in the attic above them.

There was a drop-down ladder in front of them that reached up to the attic. The ceiling fan there flap-flapped and the thump-drag sound persisted. They knew they were getting closer. They could smell victory.

Madeleine went up the ladder first. There was no light in the attic. There was only the thump-drag sound, calling invitingly to them.

"We're coming up, Stevie," Madeleine said. "We're not afraid."

She really said that, but I can tell you she'd never been so afraid in her entire life. I knew Maggie was afraid, too, since she was clutching Madeleine's ankle and wouldn't let go.

As soon as the two of them stepped off the top of the ladder, it swung up behind them and slammed shut as tightly as the front door had a few minutes earlier. A bright light came on and the ceiling fan sparked into its highest speed, stirring up a decade of dust bunnies and cobwebs.

"*Aaaarghhhh!*" said Maggie.

Madeleine dropped to the floor in a clump of nerves.

And then everything stopped. The lights went out. The fan halted. There was no more thumping, creaking, cackling, or screaming. There was only darkness and silence.

"Madeleine, are you there?" Maggie asked.

Madeleine sat up. She reached out her hand until she found Maggie. "I'm here," she said. "Are you okay?"

"Maybe. How about you?" she asked.

"Maybe," said Madeleine. "Let's get out of here."

Slowly, Madeleine got herself to her feet. It took her a few minutes to find the release for the ladder. The ladder dropped down smoothly, and in a second the girls were on the second floor of the house. They looked around. No light flickered in the mirror. No fan flapped at the window shade. The house was quiet. There was no sign of the mayhem that had so recently terrified them. It was an empty house, empty of ghosts and goblins, and mostly empty of one Stevie Lake.

It didn't take the girls long to figure out that they could leave by the back door. It opened easily, leaving the two of them standing, still terrified and confused, in the broad daylight of their very own neighborhood.

They ran around the house, across the lawn, and across the street to where their dolls, blanket, and lunch box had all been dropped. They found the blanket neatly folded and the dolls seated in a tidy row on the blanket. The lunch box had been set upright next to the blanket.

When the girls got home and walked in the door, they found the one thing they'd most feared. I was sitting at the kitchen table, having a cup of tea with Mrs. Pine and my mother.

"Oh, I hope you had a good time," I said. "I'm sorry I had to leave you, but my stomachache is almost all better now that I've had a nice hot cup of tea. Did you have fun at your party?"

Maggie, in what had become her most familiar state, could say nothing. Madeleine stammered. "Um, uh, sure. It was . . . it was . . . um, ah . . ."

"Interesting?" I suggested.

"Very," she said.

"I bet you'd like to put the dolls away now so that they don't get mussed sitting around the kitchen," I said. "Then maybe we could all climb a tree. I'm pretty sure I feel up to it."

Maggie finally said something. What she said was that she was sure her mother was expecting her home now so she couldn't stay another minute. She shoved the blanket and the dolls into Madeleine's arms and ran out the door.

"Um, I don't think I really feel like climbing a tree right now," Madeleine said. "Perhaps we could play with my dolls? Would you like to play with Elena?" she asked.

Elena, the doll that belonged in a display case, and Madeleine was offering her to me. It was a bribe and I knew it. She was trying to buy my silence because she didn't ever want her mother—or mine—to know that she and Maggie had dared me to go into the haunted house. I grinned to myself. I didn't need to play with Elena. I didn't have to play

117

with Madeleine, either. I just needed to do one more thing.

"No thanks, Maddie," I said. "I guess I'd rather just sit here for a while to be sure my stomach is really okay. I'll see you later."

She glared at me and then stormed upstairs. My victory was complete.

The rest of the visit was easy. She hardly said a word to me and I hardly said anything to her. She spent all day, every day, playing with Maggie, and I spent all my time over at the old house, by myself, reading some of the good books we'd brought along. When I wasn't there, I spent time with my mother. I actually enjoyed being by myself, and even better I enjoyed the time I spent with my mother. It was a great trip.

"What were you doing at the haunted house?" Deborah asked Stevie. "I mean, that place sounds pretty scary."

"There's no such thing as a haunted house, Deborah," Stevie said.

"But all those sounds, coming from all over the place," Deborah said. "How did that happen?"

"It's a story," Stevie said. "You don't expect me to tell you exactly everything that happened, do you?"

"Stevie!" Carole said.

"Well, it was mostly true," Stevie said. *"And the part about Madeleine and Maggie being scared out of their wits was definitely true, but the fact is they were so easy to scare that it wasn't much of a challenge."*

So, ten days later, Mom and I flew home on a plane. The trip had been good, but returning home was even better. Mad-uh-lane had been such a pain that she made Chad, Alex, and Michael look like saints. I was never so happy to see anyone in my whole life as I was to see the three of them, plus Dad, when we got home. I decided right then and there that I would never again be a bully to Michael or try to compete with Chad and Alex.

LISA, CAROLE, AND Deborah all hooted with laughter because everybody knew that Stevie rarely did anything but compete with her brothers, unless she was trying to bully them!

"Oh, go ahead and laugh," Stevie said. "I know it looks as if nothing changed, but that's not the case. The way I compete and bully since that trip is very different from the way I competed and bullied before the trip."

"Right," said Carole. "And that makes all the difference."

"But stop a minute," said Deborah. "Where's my role model for mothering? I'm supposed to expose my little child to the worst behavior in the world and see what happens?"

"Oh, no, that's not the point at all," said Stevie. "You mean you missed all the wonderful things my mother did?"

"I liked the part about hugging in her room that first night," said Deborah. "I can do that."

"Good idea," said Lisa. "Hugs are always good."

"So's encouragement," Carole agreed. "Be sure to tell your kids when they're doing something right, not just when they make mistakes."

"But there's more," said Stevie. "Lots more. First of all, my mother took me to a place where there was a kid who was so much worse than my brothers that she made them look good. There's a little reality check. Next, the part about reading out loud: Remember how much we all loved that and I especially loved the Uncle Remus tales? Remember the story about Brer Rabbit who gets caught by Brer Fox, and Brer Fox is trying to figure out the most painful way to finish off Brer Rabbit? Brer Rabbit keeps saying that Brer Fox can roast him or skin him or hang him or cut off his legs, but no matter what, he shouldn't throw him into the briar patch. Of course, that makes Brer Fox decide to throw Brer Rabbit into the briar patch. Brer Rabbit outfoxed

Brer Fox that time, because rabbits were born to live in briar patches. So he runs away, laughing at Brer Fox, and Brer Fox gets furious at him. See, that's why I begged Madeleine and Maggie not to make me go past the haunted house—because it was the one thing I wanted the very most. So be sure to read good stories about clever characters to all of your children, okay?"

"Well, I do love to read, so that will be easy," Deborah promised Stevie.

"And next, what my mother did that was wonderful was put me with the Miserable Madeleine, who was such an awful person that the only way to get back at her was to play a practical joke. I'd never played a practical joke on anyone before. Madeleine was the inspiration I needed to take up the fine art of practical joking. It's a skill I've been honing ever since."

"I'm not sure the rest of us should thank her for that," Carole said dryly. Lisa just groaned.

"And there's one more thing," said Stevie.

"Yes?" Deborah asked expectantly.

"Well, when we got back to Willow Creek, my grandmother told my mother that the best thing she could do for me was to find something that I could do that my brothers wouldn't do, something that would be mine and mine alone, something where I wouldn't be competing with my brothers at all."

"Let me guess," said Deborah. "Riding?"

Stevie smiled proudly.

"A perfect mother," Lisa said. Carole nodded. There was no disputing that.

Deborah's eyes rolled up to the ceiling. "There's no stopping you girls, is there?" she asked. "No matter what I ask you to do, you are completely incapable of telling a story that doesn't actually have to do with horses and riding."

"Well, we are The Saddle Club," Carole said. "Horses are what we like the best."

"But there was all this talk about how The Saddle Club can do anything when its members work together. So, what's so hard about just telling me a little story that isn't about riding? I'm here, doing something that's very hard for me. Seems to me that you ought to be able to do that, even though it's hard for you. It's not that I haven't enjoyed the stories you've told me, Lisa and Stevie. It's just that, well, a promise is a promise. Now I want to hear a story from Carole that doesn't even mention one word that has to do with horses." She grinned proudly because she knew it was going to be a gigantic challenge.

Lisa and Stevie both looked at Carole. Telling stories that didn't have much to do with horses had been very hard for each of them. Telling one that didn't have anything to do with horses might prove to be absolutely impossible for Carole. But it was what Deborah wanted.

"I can do it," Carole said. "I really can." And so she began.

CAROLE'S STORY

I

I CAN TELL a story that doesn't have to do with um
. . . er . . . the *h* word, but I can't tell you a story
that happened to me before I rode *h* words, because
I started doing that when I was so young that I
don't remember anything at all before that. Or
maybe I just never have considered anything that
happened before I first rode *h* words to be worth
remembering. But I will tell you something that
happened to me the summer I was nine. That
makes it nice and even, doesn't it? Lisa told a story
about when she was ten, Stevie was eight when she
met up with Madeleine, so it seems properly bal-
anced that I be nine when this happened.

This is almost as much a story about my mother
as it is about me. None of you ever knew her, and I
don't talk about her much with you. Sometimes I

think you're afraid I'll be uncomfortable talking about Mom, but really that's not the case. Dad and I talk about her often. It's a nice way of keeping our memories fresh. Even though she died a few years ago, I remember a lot of things about Mom, and most of them are really nice. I don't think I'll tell you about the time she bought me a sundress that was the wrong size or the time she tried to help me learn Roman numerals, only she got them all mixed up and I never have been able to tell the difference between D and L. Sometimes she'd forget to do things she really meant to do. There was one time she locked the keys in the trunk of the car when we were ready to leave on vacation, and she was forever forgetting to pack things she needed, like a toothbrush.

Carole had to stop her story for a few minutes because Lisa and Stevie were laughing so hard. They weren't laughing at Carole's mother, they were laughing at Carole. Forgetfulness was one of Carole's best-known traits—next to being h *word–crazy, of course.*

"All right, all right," said Carole. "So now you know that I can't help my faults. They are inherited traits!"

"Oh dear," said Deborah. "Does that mean that my child is going to make all the same mistakes I do?"

126

"Not necessarily," Stevie assured her. *"In our family, Mom and Dad are always astonished at the new kinds of mistakes my brothers and I make, so don't worry. There's hope."*

Deborah didn't seem comforted by those thoughts, but there wasn't anything Carole could do about it, so she went on with her story.

Mostly, though, my mother was wonderful. Sometimes I think I can still hear her laughter. She loved to laugh and she loved to make me and my dad laugh. It always seemed to me that when I was feeling blue, for whatever reason, Mom found a way to make me laugh and feel better. Just sitting on her lap or watching her work in the kitchen or sew on a button made me feel that I was loved and safe. Mothers can be like that, you know, only often we don't stop to think about it. Now I think about it a lot.

Mom and I spent a lot of time together when I was little. It wasn't just because I don't have brothers like Stevie—or sisters, for that matter. And it wasn't just because Mom was a stay-at-home mom like Lisa's. Even though both of those things were true, we were often together because we were sometimes the only people around that we knew.

Dad loves the Marine Corps, and Mom and I

both liked a lot of things about his job, too. One thing we all agreed on, though, was that we hated having to move, and we did a lot of that. There was a time when we were moving every three years or so, and that means that by the time I was nine, my parents and I had already lived in three places. And then the summer I was nine, we were moved to the fourth.

Most of the time when we moved, it wasn't so bad. For one thing, we were living on bases where there were other families who moved a lot, other kids who had learned to make friends quickly, other kids who knew a lot about other places. Sometimes we went to schools on the bases. More often we went to schools in the towns. I liked meeting kids who weren't Marine Corps brats, like I was, but the most important part was just meeting other kids. The problem with the move we made when I was nine was that it was just a temporary assignment for Dad. We weren't going to be there for more than three months, and it was summertime. That meant no school.

Now, I know that some people, like my friend Stevie, for instance, think the idea of no school is just about heaven, but when you've just moved to a new place, school is the fastest way to meet kids and make friends. Even tougher was the fact that the base didn't have any extra housing, so we had to rent a house off the base, where there were no other Marine Corps brats around, and, worse than that, it was way out in the country. I mean, I really actually liked all those things, except that every one of them made it impossible for me to make friends. It wasn't any better for my mom, either.

Even though we weren't there for very long, I remember that house well because it was a really nice one. It was a big old farmhouse with a huge yard and a big barn behind it. The first day we were there, I spent the whole morning just exploring the barn. It had once had a lot of animals in it—um, there might have been some you-know-whats—but definitely there had been cows and sheep. There was a chicken coop and a pen where they'd kept pigs. The old tractor was still there. The farmer who owned it was retiring, but he didn't want to sell his house yet, so he'd sold most of his farm equipment and all of his livestock and rented the house to us while he and his wife rented an apartment in Florida. They wanted to try it for three months before they sold the farm. It was a perfect deal for us all.

My room was on the second floor, down the hall from my parents' room. My window looked out over the fields. They seemed to go on for miles. When we arrived, in the early summer, they were already green with the hay that would cover them soon. I remember the smell today, sweet, moist, rich. Everything about the whole place was perfect, except for one thing: no friends.

The first few days, Mom and I spent all our time putting things away. Well, to be perfectly honest, she spent all of her time doing it, and I spent some of my time arranging my collection of model h— oops—the stuff in my room. Once I'd finished that, I explored, like the barn and the fields. There was a small pond next to the barn where I'd found some tadpoles that were just beginning to get legs. They were a little weird and very cute. I was lying on my stomach, looking into the water, when I heard my mother call me.

"I'm here, Mom," I called back.

"Carole?" She hadn't heard me.

"Here, Mom!" I called back louder.

"Where are you?" She sounded frightened.

"I'm by the pond, Mom. I'm over here." I waved to her. She didn't see me at first. She was standing by the back door of the house, with her hand shading the sun from her eyes, staring out over the miles of field and forests that surrounded our house.

There was a strong wind, tugging her dress around her and brushing her hair back. It was just a moment, but there, by the big house, with a big sky above and the wind whipping at her, she seemed terribly alone. I stood up in a hurry and called back as loudly as I could, realizing then that the wind was carrying my voice away from her instead of toward her.

"Here I am!" I ran over to her. She put her arms out and surrounded me with a hug. It felt good, but I had the funny feeling that it felt even better to her.

"Is something wrong, Mom?" I asked.

Mom shook her head. "No, dear. I just didn't know where you were and it worried me. There's so much *here* here that I don't know where here is yet."

That made me laugh. It was like Mom to say something silly like that, that still made sense.

"I was looking at little baby frogs, Mom," I told her. "They're still tadpoles. They've got the tiniest little legs and their tails are getting shorter. They are so cute! Would you like to see them?"

I was pretty sure she wouldn't. She'd been working so hard to make our new house be a real home that I thought she'd never stop working, but she surprised me because she said she wanted to see them. We lay on our stomachs together that morning, watching the tadpoles. Then a school of minnows came over to us. Mom had a biscuit left from breakfast and we gave them some crumbs. They didn't eat them, but they sure were curious about them. It was okay that they didn't eat them, because then we found an anthill in the dirt nearby, and those ants were just thrilled with a couple of crumbs.

Before I knew it, it was time for lunch, and I realized I'd spent the entire morning playing with my mother exactly the same way I would have played with my best friend. I'd had much more fun, too, because my best friend at the place we'd just moved from wouldn't have liked the idea of lying on her stomach in the mud by a pond. Mom didn't care. She knew we had a washing machine and could get clean almost as fast as we'd gotten dirty. That was the beginning of the summer when I learned that my mom was my best friend—and I was hers.

II

THE NEXT DAY it rained, so Mom and I stayed inside and played. First she taught me how to play crazy eights. It was an easy card game that I learned in a minute. It was also one where luck mattered almost as much as skill, so I could actually win some games without her letting me win. I've always hated it when adults play a game badly so that a kid can win—like we wouldn't notice.

Then it was time for lunch and Mom let me choose. We both ate peanut butter and jelly sandwiches on oatmeal bread—

"I knew she couldn't help mentioning something to do with horses," said Stevie.

"What?" Lisa asked.

"Oatmeal bread!" Stevie said. "She couldn't just have it on white bread like the rest of us?"

"Oh, hush," said Deborah. "Let her finish." The girls were a little surprised at the sharpness in Deborah's voice, but then they realized she was having another contraction. Automatically, Stevie began massaging her shoulders, Lisa dabbed at her forehead with a cool washcloth, and Carole continued her story.

—potato chips, chocolate milk, jelly beans, chocolate chips, and corn curls. Mom ate some of everything that I ate, and I think she even liked it, too. Then for dessert, I asked if we could have Rice Krispies treats. Naturally, there weren't any already in the house, so we made them. Some people might think this was an unimportant thing, but mothers are supposed to give their children some life skills, and when my mom taught me how to make Rice Krispies treats that day, she was doing us all a favor.

That afternoon, we built a little dollhouse out of some of the packing crates that we'd had from our move. All my dolls got to move into their new house at the very same time my mom and dad and I were moving into ours. It was kind of neat. By the time we were done with it, I'd decided that my dolls weren't as lucky in their new house as I was in mine, because they didn't have as good a friend as I did. My mom used an old sheet to make curtains for every single window of that cardboard dollhouse.

When I went to sleep that night, I wasn't sure if I wanted it to be rainy or sunny the next day. However it turned out to be, I just wanted to have some more fun with my mom.

I woke up very early. It was actually too early for me even to be able to tell what the weather was. It was still dark out, just a few streaks of light in the eastern sky. At first I didn't know what it was that had awakened me. I lay in bed, staring at the ceiling, thinking about the two nice days I'd had with Mom. Then I heard a noise. It wasn't a frightening noise, just a noise, and it was outside. In my hazy daze of still mostly sleeping, I was only vaguely aware of it. Then I heard it again. Something was in our backyard, below my window.

I crept out of bed. I didn't even turn on my light because it would have been too bright in the dark morning twilight. My window was open already. I pushed the curtains aside. At first, I didn't see anything. The whole backyard seemed quiet and empty. Then something moved and I heard the sound again. There, right beneath my window, was a big black dog. I guess he either heard me or saw my curtains move. I don't know which, but he looked up at me at the same instant that I spotted him. It was like our eyes met, and in an instant we knew one another. People talk about love at first sight, but I don't know about that. I just know that the second I saw that—uh—dog, we were going to be as close as could be.

I ran down the stairs and out the door to the backyard. He hadn't moved a bit. It was like he was waiting for me. He knew I'd be there and that I'd take care of him. Of course, he was right.

The first thing I wondered was if he was okay. I checked him over. There were no cuts anyplace and he didn't seem sore or bruised. He walked around just fine. In fact, he practically ran around the yard after me. It was neat. There we were. We'd just met a few minutes ago and we were already playing. Well, then I looked to see if he had anything on him that would say who he belonged to. Nothing. There was no collar, no nothing. There was just one beautiful sleek black—uh—dog. The sun came up at that moment, just peeking up over the trees of the woods. We both stopped to look at the pretty pink in the sky. Oh, I know that dogs can't see colors—actually most animals can't see colors the way people do—but they sure can see a pretty sunrise. The light of the sun reflected in the dog's shiny eyes, sparkling brightly. Then, even though I didn't know who owned him or where he'd come from or how long he'd stay with me, I did know what his name was. It was Sparkle. That was what I was going to call him, anyway. I gave Sparkle a big hug then, and I'm telling you, if he'd had arms instead of legs, he would have hugged me back.

I guess I must have been making a lot of noise with Sparkle because my dad came out into the yard to see what was up.

"Daddy, look at this beautiful dog!" I said. "His name's Sparkle. Can I keep him?"

Well, of course, everybody in the world knows exactly what Dad said then because it's what anybody would have known was the right thing to say: "A dog this friendly certainly belongs to someone, Carole. We have to find who it belongs to and give it back."

"But Dad—"

"If he were your dog, you'd want him back, wouldn't you?"

I nodded yes then, but what I was thinking was: *He is my dog. Now.*

By the time Dad left for work that morning, he and my mother had plans all set for finding what they called Sparkle's real owner. I tried very hard not to listen. I had no intention of helping them with it. I decided my job was to take care of Sparkle the best way I could. For one thing, I wanted Mom and Dad to know that when "Sparkle's real owner" couldn't be found, I'd be an ideal substitute. For another really more important thing, I wanted to take care of Sparkle because Sparkle needed to be taken care of.

I gave him water and food and I brushed his coat until it gleamed. He stood absolutely still for every second of the brushing, too. Sparkle loved it. I think my dad wouldn't have been too thrilled with the fact that I used his hairbrush to do it with, but I washed it carefully when I was done.

Then Mom picked up the telephone and began calling local vets. She figured Sparkle must live somewhere near our house and that someone would recognize him if she described him. I couldn't listen. I was so afraid that she'd find Sparkle's owner that I ran out of the house. Sparkle was there waiting for me, and I was just about certain that he was as afraid as I was that his "real owner" would come along for him. We began playing together then. We ran, we walked, we explored. We went all over the fields and all around the woods. We were inseparable.

I don't mean to make it sound like we did all of that that first morning. We didn't. It took weeks for us to go all of those places, but it had only taken one minute for us to become inseparable.

Mom and Dad kept warning me that Sparkle's real owners were bound to show up. He was a good, healthy animal and he'd been loved a lot. Maybe he'd traveled a long distance, but anyone who had owned a dog as nice as that was sure to want to find him. I guess I knew they were right about that, but every day that passed without a phone call from someone claiming to own him seemed to me like another wish fulfilled. And as more of those wishes were fulfilled, it seemed more and more possible that my biggest wish would be, too.

Oh, I dreamed a hundred different reasons why Sparkle's owners wouldn't come looking for him. Maybe his owners had been killed in a car accident. Or maybe they'd been driving on a long trip and let him out for a minute but forgot about him and went on driving. Maybe Sparkle actually belonged to the farmer who owned our house and he'd run away from Florida because it was too hot. I know these ideas of mine were a little farfetched, but I was just nine years old and I loved Sparkle very much.

III

I THINK SPARKLE loved me just as much as I loved him. We spent practically all day every day with one another. We would have been together at night, too, except Mom and Dad told me that they had promised the farmer we didn't have any pets. Sparkle stayed in the barn. He didn't seem to mind that at all. In fact, he seemed so at home there that I might have thought he'd lived there all his life. And that made *me* feel at home there.

At the same time Sparkle was making me feel at home, he was doing it for Mom, too. She made so many phone calls about him that she got to know some people that way. She ended up making friends while she did volunteer work at the animal shelter in town because of Sparkle. Sparkle made that farm a real home for both of us.

At first, as you can imagine, every time the phone rang I was afraid. I was afraid it would be someone who wanted to take Sparkle away from me. Mom had called all of our neighbors and about eight veterinarians—some in the town where our farm was and some in neighboring towns. She put an ad in our newspaper, and when nobody answered it, she put an ad in the papers in neighboring towns. Nobody called, nobody wrote, nobody came to see him. And with every day that went by, Sparkle became more and more my very own.

It seemed that we played together for hours on end. In the daytime, we were never apart. If we weren't actually going someplace together, we were staying in the yard together. I taught him things, too. He came whenever I called him, and he would do the things I asked him. He had obviously learned good manners before he came to our house, so he probably already knew most of what I said, but I could always tell that he was trying hard to please me.

One morning the phone rang and Mom answered it. By then she'd already been doing volunteer work at the animal shelter, so it didn't surprise me when the call was clearly about an animal. From her end of the conversation, I could tell that it was about an animal that had run away while it was being transported and that the transport company had been less than honest about exactly what had happened, so it wasn't easy for the owners to know where to look for it. Mom seemed pleased to be able to tell them they'd found the right place to look for their dog.

"Definitely, it's a perfect description of Midnight," she said. "Oh, I'm not surprised your daughter will be happy to have him back. A pet like that really becomes a member of the family. I can assure you, he's become one of ours."

I didn't understand at first. Mom kept looking at me and smiling. Then she covered the phone's mouthpiece and whispered excitedly to me, "His name is Midnight."

"One of the dogs at the shelter?" I asked.

She shook her head and then spoke into the phone again.

"Well, I know how much this means to Michelle, because my own daughter, Carole, has become very attached to Midnight."

Midnight? I didn't know any pet named Midnight. But then I realized suddenly that I did, in fact, know a pet named Midnight, only I called him Sparkle. This was Sparkle's owner! They'd found us and they were going to take Sparkle away.

I didn't hear any of the rest of the conversation. I was vaguely aware of the fact that Mom was making a deal to have Sparkle's owner and her father come to our house the next day to pick him up. I heard her giving them directions. I was aware then that she hung up the phone and looked toward me, smiling in that sort of sweet way that moms have of letting you know that they sympathize with the way you're feeling, but it's basically not all right. It's an "I'm sorry" and a "Please don't cry" all in one. I knew what she was going to say. She was going to tell me that Michelle loved Midnight very much and had been brokenhearted when she'd learned that he'd run off. She loved her pet every bit as much as I did, and he was her pet so I couldn't allow myself to be upset. I didn't give Mom a chance to say any of this. I just knew it was coming, and the fact that it made perfect sense was only going to upset me more. I did the only reasonable thing. I ran out toward the barn where Sparkle was patiently waiting for me. By the time I got there, I'd decided it wasn't true. There had to be some mistake. How could it be that this dog who had so quickly and so completely become my best friend actually belonged to someone else? He was mine, truly mine. Day after day, we'd proved it to one another. Nothing could change that. His name was Sparkle and he belonged to Carole Hanson. He didn't—couldn't—belong to someone named Michelle who called him Midnight.

He was waiting for me as he did every single morning, looking eagerly over the gate in the barn. His eyes lit up, as they did every morning. His tail wagged and he sniffed at me. He was mine. I patted him and hugged him. He hugged me back, I was sure.

"Oh, Sparkle," I said. "I love you." If he could have talked, I'm absolutely certain he would have said, "I love you, too."

I thought about how much this wonderful animal had come to mean to me in the last few weeks. Then I thought about another girl, someone named Michelle. She'd loved her dog, too, and I was a little bit sorry for her, but her dog was another dog. It wasn't Sparkle. It was Midnight.

143

That was the test then; I knew it. I didn't want to know, but I had to try. I took a step back and I looked the dog square in the eye.

"Midnight?" I said. He perked his head to one side and flicked his ears. His tail wagged so fast I think it was a hundred times a second.

I shouldn't have had any doubts left then. But, I told myself, it's perfectly possible that there was another dog named Midnight in his last home. Or maybe it was just the way I said it. I tried again, this time saying "Midnight" as if it were a used tissue instead of a sweet name for a black dog. Again, his tail flopped eagerly. In my heart, I knew he was excited by the name because it was his. My head, on the other hand, was still spinning with possibilities, though even then I recognized a few of them were pretty farfetched—like the idea that his previous owners only ever fed him at midnight or that it was the puppy name his mother had given him that he hadn't heard for years. By the time I was done making up possibilities, I'd convinced myself that my mother had made a terrible mistake telling these strangers to come get my dog and it was my job to save him from being taken by dognappers who would never care for him at all.

So I started making plans. I'm not very proud of this, but the fact is that I was nine years old and desperate. I had nine years worth of experience being the daughter of a Marine Corps officer. I was pretty self-sufficient. I decided this was the time to become totally self-sufficient. I would run away. I would take Sparkle with me. I really don't think I had any delusions about living on my own for very long, but I did think I would have a chance to show my parents that I was serious about keeping Sparkle and maybe that would convince them to convince Michelle and her parents that their dog had run away again and they'd have to go look for him someplace else—*anyplace* else.

It only took me a few minutes to put together my survival kit. I packed my favorite shirt, my three favorite model—um, you know, *h* words—and a copy of *Little House in the Big Woods* to help me live in the woods near our farmhouse. I know this isn't logical and I'm not particularly proud of it, but it's all true, so what can I say? I also found a bag of pretzels in the den. I guess I was expecting to live on that until I could bring in my first crops the way they did in *Little House in the Big Woods*!

145

6

"DID YOU REMEMBER your toothbrush?" Lisa asked.

"No, of course not," said Carole. "I didn't even bring a change of clothes. What good was a toothbrush going to do me, especially when there was no way I'd remember any toothpaste!"

Lisa and Stevie laughed. They looked to see if Deborah was laughing, too, but she wasn't. In fact, she wasn't even smiling. She was breathing deeply through her nose and blowing out slowly through her mouth. There was a pained look on her face. Automatically, Lisa glanced at her watch. It was only five minutes since the last contraction.

Lisa took one of Deborah's hands and held it

while Stevie put a cool, damp washcloth on her forehead. Carole helped Deborah concentrate on her breathing.

"In-two-three-four, out-two-three-four-five-six."

She had to do that five times. That was more than for the previous contractions. Most of them had been no more than three or four breaths. The girls looked at one another.

"They're getting longer," Stevie observed.

Deborah nodded.

"And closer together," said Lisa.

Deborah nodded again. Then she released a final breath.

"All done," she said.

"Is it time to call the doctor again?" Lisa asked.

Deborah frowned. "It can't be," she said. "This is supposed to take twenty hours. It hasn't been anywhere near that long. And besides, my contractions aren't that close together yet."

"Well, that was five minutes," Lisa said.

"It couldn't have been," Deborah said. "You must have measured wrong.

"It sure was—" Stevie began.

Lisa cut her off, though. "We probably did measure wrong," she said. "We'll be more careful next time. Gee, I could use another cup of tea, and Deborah's ice chips are all gone. Stevie, come help me in the kitchen, will you?"

"You don't need any help getting tea," Stevie said. "I think I'd better stay here with Deborah."

"I don't remember where the kettle is," said Lisa. "You're the one who found it in the first place, Stevie," she said.

Stevie's look showed her irritation. The kettle was right on the stove in plain sight. Then it dawned on her that Lisa actually had something else in mind. Her hints really weren't all that subtle. Stevie abandoned her annoyance and stood up.

"Good idea," she said. "I could use another cup of tea myself."

"We'll be right back," Lisa assured Carole and Deborah.

"Don't go anywhere," Stevie joked.

Deborah closed her eyes. Carole nodded. She knew what her friends were up to. It was time to call the doctor again, and if Deborah didn't know it, The Saddle Club did. They'd call him from the kitchen.

Lisa sighed with relief when she spotted the Redial button on the phone. The last person to use the phone had been Deborah, and the last person she'd called had been her doctor. They didn't have to search for a number.

The doctor's nurse answered on the third ring. It took Lisa a few seconds to explain to the nurse who she was and why she was calling.

"Right, Deborah Hale. She's having a baby."

"All of Dr. Husted's patients are having babies," the nurse answered. "Dr. Husted is an obstetrician."

Briefly, Lisa wondered if doctors' nurses were required to have brains, and it occurred to her to ask the question. She decided that wouldn't help. She returned to the reason for her call.

"No, I mean, like *now*," Lisa said. "Today, soon, very soon." She made a face at Stevie to indicate that she was dealing with someone who wasn't getting the point.

"Hale . . . Hale . . . um . . . uh . . . Hale," said the nurse.

"Regnery?" Lisa suggested. Since she was Max's wife, that was her married name, but she always used her maiden name as far as the girls knew.

"Regnery . . . Regnery . . . um . . . uh . . . Regnery," said the nurse. "Oh, right, Mrs. Regnery. Well, she's not due for another couple of weeks. I'm afraid you'll have to get any information on her condition from her or from her husband. I'm certainly not allowed to discuss a patient's condition without her specific authorization."

"No, you don't understand," Lisa said, mustering every ounce of patience she could. "I don't want you to discuss the patient's condition. *I'm* discussing the patient's condition. I'm telling you that Mrs. Regnery is going to have a baby. She is in labor and her contractions are now five minutes apart. When she spoke to her doctor a couple of hours ago, he said to call when the contractions were five minutes apart. We're calling to tell you that. Now."

"Oh," said the nurse. "I see. You mean the baby seems to be on its way."

"Yes," said Lisa. She sighed with relief. "Maybe I should speak with the doctor?"

"Yes, I think that would be a good idea," said the nurse. "At the moment, he's in surgery, but I'll let him know as soon as he can be reached. You know, this is Mrs. Regnery's first baby and the labor is liable to be quite long. You shouldn't worry. The contractions could remain at five-minute intervals for a good long time. You should stay with her and let her know that you've called the doctor, and you should call back here in case there's any change. Okay?"

"Okay," Lisa said. She felt a little better, but not a lot. She told Stevie what the nurse had said.

"I guess they know what they're doing," Stevie said. "And I'm sure she can reach Dr. Husted if she has to. In the meantime, there's someone else we need to reach."

"Max," said Lisa.

"Right." Fortunately, both Max and his mother had been talking about the Pony Club workshop for some time and the girls knew where it was. Stevie made the call. It was no more productive than the call to Dr. Husted's office had been. It turned out that the workshop had moved from the conference center to a stable and that all the participants would be leaving directly from there.

"Soon?" Stevie asked.

"Pretty soon," the woman said.

That was too vague. Stevie realized that Max really needed to know what was going on. He would want to be here. He should be here. She explained to the woman what was going on and asked her if she could get a message to Max that he should call home. She said she'd be glad to do that.

Lisa and Stevie felt that they'd done the right thing all around. They poured more water in the

151

teapot and took the tray and some ice chips back into the living room.

The woman at the Pony Club workshop was as good as her word. Minutes later, the phone rang and Deborah picked it up.

"Max?" she said. "Oh, sure, I'm fine. No, no problems. Well, they didn't need to do that. You know this is going to take a long time. There's no hurry. You finish up the workshop. The girls are taking great care of me. In fact, I think I've got them doing all the work in this labor! They seem to like it better than mucking out stables!"

The Saddle Club could hear Max laughing at the other end of the phone. On the one hand, they were glad that Deborah felt good enough to reassure him. On the other, they were relieved when they could tell that Max was insisting he and his mother would leave the conference and come home.

"Okay, I'll see you in about two hours," Deborah said. She gave him a kiss over the phone and hung up.

"Is that what the kettle argument was about?" she asked, looking suspiciously at Lisa and Stevie.

"Yeah," Stevie said. "We really thought he ought to know."

"Max put us in charge," Lisa reminded Deborah. "And he would have blamed us for not calling."

"Well, maybe you're right," Deborah said. "He'll want to be here. But I hope he doesn't get here before you all finish your stories. I'm enjoying every word of these horseless tales! In fact, I'd enjoy them even more if I could stretch out on my bed. Do you girls mind if we move the party upstairs?"

The Saddle Club glanced at each other nervously. Deborah must be getting tired from the contractions—more tired than they thought.

"Well?" she said, lumbering to her feet. Lisa and Carole each grabbed an arm and Stevie followed with the tea. Deborah huffed as she took the steps slowly. When she was settled in her bed, she gave the girls a big smile.

"Aaah, that's better," she said. "Now, Carole, where were you?"

CAROLE'S STORY, CONTINUED

IV

RIGHT, WELL, THERE I was with my book, a few clothes, and some pretzels. I snuck out of the house, got Sparkle from the barn where he was waiting for me, and off we went. Although we were living in a farmhouse and there were lots of fields there, I knew we'd be spotted very quickly in the fields. Besides, it was *Little House in the Big Woods* that I had brought, not *Little House on the Prairie*. So, we headed for the woods.

I guess it must have been about four o'clock in the afternoon when we left the farm. By five, I was exhausted from walking. Even Sparkle seemed a little tired, so I sat down and he stayed right next to me. Naturally, all that walking had made me hungry. I broke out the bag of pretzels. They didn't last long. I think I finished them off in about ten minutes. Of course, I hadn't brought anything to drink, and there's nothing worse than eating salty pretzels and not having anything to drink—well, maybe chocolate chip cookies without milk, but you know what I mean. I was really thirsty and I knew Sparkle had to be, too. He'd shared the pretzels with me. We had to find something to drink, and the obvious choice was water. Since I had no idea where there might be any water, I had to keep going. I couldn't go back—there wasn't any point, because I knew there was no water that way except at the house.

Sparkle and I walked for another hour, maybe more. The sun was still out, but it was beginning to drop toward the trees, and in the forest it was getting darker. I looked at my watch then. I couldn't believe it was only six o'clock. It was the middle of summer and it should have been light at six. But it wasn't. It was almost as dark as night, and I didn't know why—until the first flash of lightning. It startled me so much that I just about screamed. Sparkle was just as surprised as I was and he jumped about six inches—but not nearly as far as he and I both did when the thunder came. It was a horrendous noise. It seemed like it was right next to me, as loud as anything I've ever heard in my whole life. I grabbed Sparkle for comfort. He kept moving away, and I thought he was trying to pull away from me. He yanked so hard at my arms that I had to let go. I didn't know then, but he was trying to tell me something. I found out soon enough, though.

There was a terrible cracking and ripping sound above my head. It wasn't like the thunder or any sound I'd ever heard before. I looked up just in time to see a big branch of the tree tumbling down—right above where I was standing. I remember it now as clearly as if it had happened only a second ago. The big branch broke its way through the lower branches of the tree, ripping at the leaves and cracking the twigs. I stood there, too scared to move, and it was too late anyway. It was an enormous branch and I never could have gotten out of its way in time. Maybe it's better that I didn't try, because if I'd been anywhere but where I was, I might have been crushed very badly.

As it was, the branch knocked me down. I was stunned when I hit the ground. I tried to sit up and look around, but I couldn't move because the branch was on top of me and I couldn't see anything but leaves, everywhere.

"Sparkle? Are you there?"

He barked loudly to answer me. I couldn't see where he was, but I could hear him moving, so I knew he was okay. Also, the sounds he made were perfectly normal.

Once I knew he was all right, I had to figure out if I was all right. I had a couple of scrapes and bruises, but I didn't think it was any worse than that. I could move my arms and wiggle my toes. The thing I couldn't do, though, was stand up or pull myself out from under the branch. It was almost as big as a tree and I was completely pinned down. I was, in a word, stuck.

I think what happened next is what's sometimes called shock. Sparkle was okay. I was okay. I knew I was okay. But I also knew it had been a very near thing. If I'd been a foot to the left or to the right, I might not have been okay. I might have been hit in the head with the branch. I might have been paralyzed or killed. I remember those thoughts going through my head and I remember that I didn't want to think about them. Then I don't remember anything for a long time after that. I guess I sort of fainted.

When I woke up, it was raining. I was grateful then for all the leaves on the branch. They didn't exactly keep me dry, but they did keep me from

getting totally soaked. It took me a minute to remember where I was and why I was there. The fact
that I couldn't move at all reminded me of everything.

"Sparkle!" I called out.

There was no answer. I called him again and
again. Still there was no answer. No matter how
loudly I called his name, he didn't answer.

I took a deep breath. "Midnight!" I called out.
The only answer I heard was silence. I was stuck, I
was alone, and I was wet. Plus, of course, I was hungry, cold, and afraid. It wasn't long before I was
crying, too. I cried until I finally fell asleep from
exhaustion.

When I woke up again, it was dark in the woods,
but it had stopped raining and I could see some
light from the sky above me. At least that's where I
thought it was coming from. Then I heard something. It took me a minute to realize it was the
sound of Sparkle barking.

"Sparkle?" I cried out.

"Carole?" came the answer.

Now, I don't want you to get the idea that the
dog had learned how to talk in the thunderstorm.
No, it wasn't Sparkle who answered me. It was

Mom, and the sound of her voice in those dark woods was the sweetest sound I'd ever heard!

We kept calling each other until she and Dad found me. Somehow they managed to work their way through the thick leaves of the branch, and both of them gave me a hug at the same time. Nothing ever felt so good.

It took me a bit of work to convince them that I was okay except for being pinned under the branch.

"Don't worry, honey," Dad said. "I'll move that thing for you."

Now, I've never understood how he did it. Even though I was just a kid, I was pretty strong, and I hadn't been able to move the darn thing one teeny tiny bit. Dad looked at me, then he looked at the branch. He reached down under it with one hand, bent his knees to brace himself, and then stood, lifting the branch right up off me.

"This way, dear," my mother said, helping me out of the trap that had held me prisoner for so many hours. And then I was free.

Well, we all cried then. We hugged one another and then we cried some more. It was only after about our fifteenth hug and fourteenth cry that I asked them how on earth they had found me.

"Sparkle showed us the way," said Mom.

I realized then that that wonderful dog, my very best friend, hadn't abandoned me at all. He'd had the good sense to go get my parents and had brought them there to rescue me!

So, we had our fifteenth cry and our sixteenth hug, only this time we all hugged Sparkle, too.

It was time to go home then. We walked back to our farmhouse, and after a nice warm bath, I got into bed and slept and slept and slept.

I remember feeling this wonderful feeling of being safe and being loved and knowing that those were the two most important feelings in the world.

What I don't remember is knowing that Sparkle's real owners were coming the next day to pick him up.

I WAS IN my room when the Lefferts' car pulled into our driveway. I couldn't see it. I just heard it because the car doors slammed so loudly. Then a voice called out, "Midnight!"

Sparkle was inside the barn, but I could hear him bark loudly in response. He knew the name; he knew the voice. I looked out the window.

Michelle ran across our backyard to our barn. Sparkle jumped over the gate that was supposed to hold him in the barn and ran to greet her. His tail wagged a zillion times a second, and I think he licked every single inch of her face. She hugged him and buried her face in his soft fur. I knew she was crying because she was so happy to see her dog again.

Then her father came into the yard. My mother was next to him, showing him the way, I guess. He stopped about ten feet away from where Michelle was hugging the dog and he watched. I saw him sigh then, as if his shoulders were collapsing, and he bent his head down. He was crying. I guess it was relief or joy or both or I don't know what, but he cried.

The next thing I knew, my mother was crying as well. Then she gave Mr. Leffert a little hug. It was a sweet gesture—two strangers sharing a special moment—and it had a strange effect on me. It made me cry, too.

So there we were, four people and a dog, all crying our eyes out. I never felt so confused in my whole life. I was crying because I knew I was going to lose Sparkle and I was crying because it made me so happy that Michelle and Midnight were back together again. Believe me, crying because you're happy and miserable at the same time is a very confusing business.

Eventually I went downstairs and met Michelle.

Part of me wanted her to be an awful pain, but of course it turned out she was as nice as could be. Anybody who owned a dog as nice as Sparkle/Midnight had to be nice.

Fortunately, Michelle and her father had to go quickly. They had a long drive to their new home. That was okay as far as I was concerned. I didn't want Sparkle to leave, but I also couldn't stand waiting for it to happen.

That night, when Dad came home for dinner, we talked about everything that had happened. My parents weren't anywhere near as angry with me as I think they might have been, or as I was afraid they would be. I'd frightened them by running off, but they sort of understood. They were awfully glad that Sparkle had known how to find them and show them where I was, and we talked about what a wonderful pet he was and what a wonderful time I'd had with him.

Then Dad told Mom and me the most exciting news. He'd finally heard about his transfer. The Marine Corps wanted him to go to Quantico right near Washington, D.C. He'd been promised that this would be a long assignment, probably his last move. Dad said it meant we could really settle down. We could buy our very own house in a town, and I could go to the town school and not worry about moving anywhere before the end of the school year. We'd have our own backyard. Dad told us that he knew there was a nice town near Quantico called Willow Creek, Virginia. He'd even heard about a house there . . .

"Mom," I said, but I was so excited I could hardly talk. She didn't hear me. So I tried again. "Mom," I practically croaked.

"Yes, Carole," said my mother.

"When we have our own house in our own town where I can have friends and we can live for a long time, can we, I mean, can I—please? Can I have a dog just like Sparkle for my very own?"

Mom smiled at me then. "Yes, dear. Your father and I have already decided that you will never be far from the animals you love. I promise you that one day, very soon, you will have your very own pet to love and care for just as you did Sparkle. Only this time, don't run away, okay?"

"Okay," I agreed.

Mom and Dad kept their promise, too. And so did I.

"OH, CAROLE, THAT was a lovely story!" Deborah said.

Carole was very pleased that Deborah had liked it so much.

"And she hardly mentioned horses at all!" Stevie said.

"Right, well there was that stuff about the model *h* words," Lisa reminded her. "But, then, nobody's perfect."

"More than that, she gave me some great ideas about what good parenting is," said Deborah.

"Definitely, the part about not having a fit just because she did something stupid and dangerous like running away and letting a tree fall on her," Stevie said. "Personally, I think all parents should take a page out of that book. Carole, maybe you could tell my parents about how they should behave in case I ever do something just a little bit, oh, I don't know, should I say 'impetuous'? Actually, I definitely should say *impetuous* because that's the word my parents are forever using—once they got tired of saying *harebrained*. It's not my favorite word, though maybe that's just because I hear it so often. 'Oh, Stevie, you're so impetuous.' It's not fair, you know. It's not even true. *Impetuous* is when you don't think about what you are doing. The fact is that I really think a lot about all those wild and crazy things I do. Anyway, Deborah, it's important to recognize your child's strengths and to appreciate them. Deborah? Deborah?"

All three girls looked at Deborah now. She hadn't heard a word Stevie was saying. She was doing her breathing exercises and it didn't look as if they were really helping her.

"Do you think maybe we'd better call the doctor again?" Lisa asked. Carole and Stevie nodded.

"I'll stay here with Deborah," Carole said. "You two go make the call. I know we've never seen a baby born before, but we've certainly seen mares deliver foals, and if Deborah were a mare, I'd say she was pretty close to delivering her foal."

Lisa and Stevie hurried back downstairs. Stevie dialed Dr. Husted's number once more, and once more the doctor's nurse answered.

"No, I'm afraid that Dr. Husted is still in surgery," the nurse said. "It's an emergency, you know."

"So is this," said Stevie. "Mrs. Regnery is about to have her baby."

"Yes, I'm sure," said the nurse.

Stevie could tell from the nurse's tone that she wasn't at all sure. It was more than a little frustrating for her to have someone distrust her so much on the phone—especially someone who had never even met her!

She asked the nurse to let Dr. Husted know that they had called and that they were sure he ought to know Deborah was really about to have a baby.

"I'll let him know as soon as he calls me," said the nurse.

Stevie practically slammed down the phone. Carole joined them in the kitchen then. "She's had another contraction," she told her friends. "This time, it was just a minute since the last one. I'm telling you, she's about to have that baby, for sure."

166

"I don't know what to do," Stevie said. "Up until now, I've been pretty sure that everything we were doing for Deborah was good for her. Telling her stories is one thing, but delivering a baby is another altogether."

"We need help," Lisa agreed. "Maybe we should just call an ambulance."

"Good idea," said Carole, reaching for the phone. But before she could dial, a set of headlights appeared in the driveway. It was the first time any of the three of them had noticed that it was late enough to be dark. They'd been with Deborah for more than five hours!

"Maybe it's the doctor," said Stevie.

"Maybe it's Max," said Lisa.

"Look, it's Judy!" said Carole. "Isn't that wonderful?"

Stevie shook her head in amazement. "How can you possibly be thinking about Patch's leg at a time like this?"

Lisa laughed. "Don't be silly, Stevie," she said. "She's not thinking about Patch, she's thinking about the fact that we now have an adult here with us, somebody that Dr. Husted's nurse will listen to. Right?"

"Sort of," Carole said. "Come on. I'll go get her

before she gets to Patch's stall. You two stay with Deborah."

Carole hurried out the kitchen door of the Regnerys' house. She was only vaguely aware of the cool evening air that brushed her skin while she ran toward the stable. What was on her mind was a woman who needed help and three girls who seemed unable to help her. It wasn't easy to admit that there were things The Saddle Club couldn't do, but she guessed that if she had to make a list, delivering babies would probably have to be on it.

"Judy!" she called out down the long hall of the stable.

"Is that you, Carole?" Judy answered from around a corner. "Boy, this place is quiet. I figured that when Max left The Saddle Club in charge, there would be some sort of disaster going on that I'd have to sort out, but if I don't count the fact that Nickel's stall really needs a mucking out—"

"Judy, there *is* a problem," Carole said.

"I know. Patch's leg. Well, this old boy's had sore ankles before, and he'll have them again. I see that you wrapped it—"

"Not Patch," said Carole. "It's Deborah."

"She's got a sore leg, too?" Judy teased.

"It's not a joke," said Carole. "She's going to have a baby."

"Of course she is. Everybody knows that. That's what that enormous belly—"

"No, I mean soon," said Carole. "Like *now*. Her contractions are less than a minute apart, and every time we've talked to her doctor's office, the nurse says the doctor's in emergency surgery. We were just about to call an ambulance, but maybe you can help."

"One minute apart, did you say?" Judy asked.

"Yep," Carole said. "We've been timing them. I know this should be taking longer. Even Deborah doesn't believe it. That's why we've been calling her doctor for her."

Judy picked up the medical bag she'd dropped next to Patch's stall. "Carole, what are we doing standing here and talking? Let's go to the house. I'll see Deborah, and then I'll get that doctor's attention, one way or another!"

The two of them ran back through the kitchen door and hurried upstairs. They found Lisa and Stevie each holding Deborah's hands while Deborah puffed away with her breathing exercises.

"You're about to have a baby, aren't you?" Judy asked.

Deborah nodded.

"Girls, get me some clean towels and some boiling water to sterilize my instruments."

"Should we call an ambulance?" Lisa asked.

"Yes," said Judy. "But I have a feeling this baby isn't waiting for any ambulance."

The next few minutes were extremely busy for The Saddle Club. Lisa brought a large pot of boiling water up to Deborah's room; Stevie gave Judy a stack of clean towels; Carole carried in a pan of lukewarm water and some soap.

"I think you'd better leave us alone now," said Judy. "But when you go downstairs, you might just call Dr. Husted's nurse one more time."

Stevie, Carole, and Lisa all hurried downstairs. Carole made the call this time. The nurse said she'd page Dr. Husted and phone for an ambulance.

It was strange. A few minutes earlier there had been a lot of activity with a lot of things to do. Now Judy was here, Deborah was about to have her baby, and there was nothing to do.

"A whole new life is starting upstairs, right now," Lisa said. "Isn't that strange?"

"Newborns are mostly wrinkly and red," said Stevie. "This one probably will be, too."

"Not like horses," Carole remarked. "Newborn foals are totally cute from the very instant they are born—or at least as soon as they start to stand up and walk around."

"This baby will take a whole year or more before he can walk," said Stevie.

"But it's a whole human being," said Lisa. "Wrinkly, scrinchy, red-faced, and dependent though he may be right now, he will grow up, learn to walk, talk—"

"And ride," said Carole.

"He'll have his own life," said Lisa.

"Maybe even some brothers," said Stevie. She made a face to let her friends know that she wouldn't wish that on Deborah and Max's son. "But just think how much money we can make baby-sitting!" Stevie said. Money was a constant worry for Stevie. The problem was that she spent it as fast as she earned it, and if she earned extra money baby-sitting, she found extra ways to spend it. "But then, Max barely trusts us with the horses; imagine what we'd have to do to convince him that we could look after his son!"

"Hopes, dreams, everything," said Lisa. "A complete life. Isn't it unbearably exciting?"

That was, of course, exactly what it was—unbearably exciting. For months they'd known this baby was coming. They had thought about it ever since Max and Deborah got married. And now the time was here and somehow all of their anticipation wasn't the same as the actual fact.

Stevie glanced at the ceiling. Deborah's room was right above the kitchen. Carole and Lisa looked up as well. There were no sounds from above, no way of knowing what was going on.

"I hope she's okay," said Stevie.

"Millions of babies get born every year," Lisa said sensibly.

"She's in good hands," said Carole.

Carole looked at her own hands. Then she reached out with them, one to each of her best friends. Lisa took one, Stevie the other, then Lisa and Stevie held hands. They made a circle—a circle of friendship, of hope, of support, and they sat there quietly, listening for any sound, any hint of what was happening, and any cry for help. If Judy or Deborah needed them, they'd be there in a second.

Among three girls who loved to talk, it seemed a little strange to sit silently, but they knew that they were each listening for a new voice, a new life.

And, as Judy promised, it didn't take long.

The silence in the kitchen was pierced by a tiny, insistent wail. It stopped for a second and then resumed.

"It's a baby!" Stevie said.

8

THE THREE GIRLS jumped up out of their seats and ran to the stairs.

"We did it!" said Stevie as they fled up the stairs, taking them two at a time.

"Judy did it," Carole corrected her.

"Deborah did it," Lisa said sensibly.

Of course, Lisa was right. Now the question remained, what exactly had Deborah done? Could they see her? Could they see the baby?

They stopped at the door to Deborah's room. Lisa knocked.

"Come on in," Judy said.

They entered. Judy was washing her hands and

174

instruments in the hot water Lisa had brought up. Deborah sat on the bed, looking extremely tired but happy. In her arms was a tiny little bundle, wrapped in a clean towel and making the most amazing gurgling sounds.

The girls tiptoed over and peered at the bundle. Deborah lifted the corner of the towel over her baby's face. The face was round with big blue eyes and tiny thin little eyebrows, a perfect little nose, and a sweet mouth that opened to reveal pink gums. The baby's eyes blinked in the bright light and then closed in a contented sleep.

"Ooooh," said Lisa, breathless with excitement.

"Cute!" said Stevie. "And so tiny!"

"It'll be a couple of years before that one gets into a saddle," said Carole.

"Someone's coming," said Judy, looking out the window. "Why don't you go see who it is? It's probably the ambulance. You can show them the way up here. Mother and baby seem to be doing fine, but there's no harm in having a people doctor's opinion on the subject!"

The girls hurried downstairs, expecting to see flashing lights. What they saw, instead, was Max and Mrs. Reg hurrying in from their car.

175

There was a worried look on Max's face. "Is she okay?" Max asked.

"Did the ambulance come?" asked Mrs. Reg.

"She's fine and the ambulance hasn't come yet," said Lisa. "In fact, it should be here in a minute, but Judy said she's sure they're both okay."

"Did I hear you say '*both* okay'?" said Max.

"Yeah, both," said Stevie.

"You mean both Judy and Deborah?" asked Mrs. Reg.

"Nope, well, Judy's fine, too," Carole assured them.

"We mean both Deborah and the baby."

"The baby came already?" Mrs. Reg said breathlessly. "Did you hear that Max? You're a father!"

"That's right!" said Carole. "Max the Fourth is here, safe and sound."

"And cute," said Stevie.

"Adorable," said Lisa. But they each knew it was unlikely that Max the Third heard any of what they'd said. He was running into the house and up the stairs faster than they'd ever seen him do anything. Mrs. Reg was no slouch in the rushing department. She was right behind him. Stevie, Carole, and Lisa weren't far behind.

"Deborah? Deborah!" he cried loudly. "Are you okay?"

"I'm fine," she said calmly. "Come meet our baby."

The three girls and Mrs. Reg watched from the door. It was as if Max couldn't run anymore, or he didn't want to run. He didn't want to upset his newborn baby or his wife.

"Oh, Deborah!" he said when he saw the baby's sweet, perfect face. He looked at his wife with love and adoration, and everyone in the room understood his joy and his pride at knowing that together they had created this precious life.

Then, with a big, beaming smile on his face, he uttered the words everybody had expected for eight months: "Maximilian Regnery the Fourth!" he declared.

"Um, Max, I'm not so sure about that," said Deborah.

"But I thought we'd decided," said Max.

"Well, I know, but—"

"It's not just about me," said Max. "It's the whole line of Regnerys—my dad, my grandfather. I've always known I'd have a baby named Maximilian the Fourth. Why do you have a problem with it?"

"Well, I don't, really," said Deborah, looking adoringly at the baby in her arms. "But I think some of her classmates may think it's a little odd."

"Oh, kids'll find all kinds of things to make fun of. I got jokes about being named—um—*her*?"

"Meet your *daughter*," Deborah said. "Max, it's a filly, not a colt."

"G-Girl?" Max stammered. "I never expected a girl."

"Are you disappointed?" Deborah asked, suddenly concerned.

"Oh, no. Not at all!" said Max. "I like girls. Actually, I like some girls a lot—as long as they don't talk in class and get all their chores done and don't cause too much trouble at Pony Club meetings. Sure, girls are fine. But they aren't named Maximilian."

"Definitely," Deborah agreed.

"They are named other things, like, uh . . ."

"Lisa," Carole suggested.

Stevie offered another possibility. "Carole," she said.

"Mrs. Reg," suggested Lisa.

That made everybody laugh.

"Anything but Stephanie," said Stevie.

There was a moment of quiet.

"How about—" said Lisa.

"I've got an idea," said Carole.

"You know what?" said Stevie.

The girls looked at one another. They knew perfectly well that they had all had exactly the same idea at the same time, so they spoke together, in unison:

"Maxine!"

"I like it," said Deborah.

"So do I," said Max.

"It would mean that you'd never have to saddle a son with the name Maximilian," said Mrs. Reg.

Max looked at his mother in surprise. "You mean you don't like my name?" he asked.

"I loved your father very, very much," she said, and that seemed like a complete answer to the question.

Deborah and Max looked at their tiny little daughter. "Maxine Hale Regnery," Max said. Deborah smiled. "No numbers—just a name. It's a beautiful name."

"For a beautiful baby," said Deborah.

"Is somebody here about to have a baby?"

There at the door to the room stood two emergency medical technicians, one tall, carrying a medical kit, and one short, holding a stretcher.

"Not for a long time," said Deborah.

Everybody laughed.

"Oh, dear, that's another one we missed," said the tall man to his partner.

"Did you manage okay on your own?" the short one asked.

"I was hardly alone," said Deborah. "I had three fine helpers through most of my labor, and then the doctor arrived just in time to deliver the baby."

The technician put down his medical bag. "I thought they told us there was no doctor here. We wouldn't have rushed if we'd known—"

It took a few minutes to straighten out the situation. The men from the ambulance had never heard of a vet delivering a baby, but it was clear from the robust and happy condition of Maxine that Judy had done an excellent job. The technicians checked Maxine over carefully and assured everybody that she was as fit as could be. There was no need to take her or Deborah to the hospital, though it would probably be a good idea to have Dr. Husted stop by within a day or so.

Stevie suspected that Dr. Husted would be as much use now that Maxine was born as he had been while she was *being* born. She was about to say as much when Deborah announced that she was extremely tired and would appreciate it if everybody, except Max and Maxine, would leave her alone.

Judy said she still had to check on Patch's leg, and then she'd be glad to drop The Saddle Club off at Stevie's house, where they were having a sleepover. It wasn't a long walk to Stevie's, but they were tired. The girls were glad for the offer. Before they left, they asked if they could come back the next day to visit Maxine.

"Could I stop you?" Max asked.

"No," they said in chorus.

He hugged all three of them at the same time and thanked them for taking such good care of Deborah.

181

9

THERE WAS A flurry of activity at Pine Hollow when the girls got there in the morning. The stable had gotten little attention the previous day, since Max, his mother, and Red had all been away.

"What can we do, Mrs. Reg?" Carole asked when they arrived.

"Well, there are plenty of chores to do, and I'd like to give you a list, but Max told me he wanted to see the three of you right away when you arrived. He's upstairs with Deborah. So go on up. Hurry, now."

"Right away!" Carole said, echoing Mrs. Reg's words. The three of them trooped up the stairs, remembering that it hadn't been so many hours ago that they'd run up the stairs to meet Maxine for the first time. The door was ajar. They knocked softly to announce their arrival and then went in.

Max was sitting on a chair next to the bed, holding Deborah's hand. Maxine was in a bassinet on the other side of the bed. The girls peered into the bassinet to see their newest friend sound asleep.

"You wanted to see us, Max?"

"Well, really, I'm the one who wanted to see you," said Deborah. "I don't know how I could have made it through everything that happened yesterday without the three of you. You just seemed to know exactly what to do, how to do it, and when to do it. I've been telling Max about the ice chips and the massages and the hand-holding. This morning, when I talked to Dr. Husted, he told me how you'd called his nurse to tell her what was going on—and you'll be interested to know that what's going on with her right now is that she's looking for a new job—and you were totally wonderful!"

"We were just glad to be helpful," said Lisa.

"You were more than that. You were even considerate. I haven't told Max about how you entertained me."

"What did they do, tell you the plots of every horse book they'd ever read?" Max joked.

"Not at all!" Deborah said. "Though, not surprisingly, they did offer. No, well, you know, I like horses and all, I mean a bit, but sometimes it's nice to hear about something else. I asked if each of them would tell me a story about their own lives that didn't have to do with horses."

"These three?" Max asked, astonished. "You mean they each actually managed that?"

"Well, sort of," Deborah said. "Lisa's story didn't have to do with horses, and neither did Stevie's, but the fact was that each of the stories led up to their parents' allowing—or encouraging—them to learn to ride. They were nice stories, to be sure, but it wasn't one hundred percent what I'd asked for."

"And Carole's was about nothing but horses, right?" Max asked.

"Not a bit of it!" said Deborah. "That was the real surprise. She told us all about this wonderful dog named Sparkle who got lost and Carole and her mother took care of it until its owner came, but not before the brave little dog saved Carole's life and how her parents promised her that after that they would buy her a dog of her very own. It was the sweetest story, Max. And I'd never known Carole was so devoted to dogs!"

Stevie snorted. Lisa giggled. Max just laughed.

"Oh, come on, guys," said Carole. "It was the best I could do!"

"It was a great story. It really touched me," said Deborah.

"Me too," Lisa said through her laughter.

"Oh, I loved it!" Stevie agreed. "And it was all new to me, too!"

"Right!" said Max. The three of them laughed together.

"Carole, why are they making fun of you?" Deborah asked. "Wasn't your story true?"

"Every word of it," Carole said.

"Carole!" said Stevie.

"Well, almost every word of it," Carole said.

"Carole!" Lisa said.

"Well, every word except one," Carole said.

"Which word wasn't true?" Deborah asked.

"Um . . . uh . . . well . . . *dog*," said Carole.

Deborah got it and started laughing then, too. "Does this, by any chance, mean that Sparkle wasn't a dog?" she asked.

185

"Uh . . . yes," Carole admitted.

"Is it just possible that Sparkle was a horse?" she asked.

"Not exactly," said Carole.

"Carole, don't split hairs," Max told her.

"Okay, well, right. Sparkle was a pony," she said.

"I knew it was too good to be true," Deborah said, teasing the girls. "You couldn't possibly talk that long without talking about horses! The trouble with being married to a horseman is that everything has to do with horses! I go through labor listening to three stories that are all about horses, and then my baby is delivered by an equine veterinarian!"

"But they were good stories," Carole said. "And we did try to give you some ideas about being a good mother. In my story, for instance, my parents were good to their word. As soon as we moved into our house in Willow Creek, I started taking lessons with Max and riding here. My mother had promised me my very own horse, and although she didn't live long enough to see me get him, Dad bought me Starlight with money she'd left me, so she fulfilled her promise. That's really important. When you make a promise, it's got to be for real, especially when it matters a lot—like a promise about getting a horse."

186

"You're right," said Deborah. "All of your stories had good lessons in them for me. I'll try to be the best mother I can. Now, how can Max and I thank you for everything you did yesterday?"

"Will you let us baby-sit Maxine?" Stevie asked.

"Great idea!" said Lisa.

"Really soon!" said Carole.

"Sure," Deborah agreed. "Are you that eager to earn some money?" she asked.

"Oh, no, it's not that," said Lisa. "I mean, we were talking about this last night at Stevie's house. We'll let you pay us—if you want to, that is."

"We just want to spend time with Maxine," said Stevie.

"Well, we sort of have to," Carole said.

"Why 'have to'?" asked Max.

"Easy," said Stevie. "She's already been voted in as the newest member of The Saddle Club!"

Deborah shook her head. "My daughter can't even burp properly and she's already fated to be horse-crazy!"

"Lucky girl," said Carole.

Lisa and Stevie couldn't have said it better.

ABOUT THE AUTHOR

BONNIE BRYANT is the author of many books for young readers, including novelizations of movie hits such as *Teenage Mutant Ninja Turtles* and *Honey, I Blew Up the Kid,* written under her married name, B. B. Hiller.

Ms. Bryant began writing The Saddle Club in 1986. Although she had done some riding before that, she intensified her studies then and found herself learning right along with her characters Stevie, Carole, and Lisa. She claims that they are all much better riders than she is.

Ms. Bryant was born and raised in New York City. She still lives there, in Greenwich Village, with her two sons.

Don't miss Bonnie Bryant's next exciting Saddle Club adventure . . .

SADDLE SORE
The Saddle Club #66

The girls of The Saddle Club and their friend Emily have headed West to the Bar None Ranch. Emily has cerebral palsy, and she's helping the ranch's owner make it accessible to riders with special needs. Then they meet a girl their own age at the ranch. She's a former rider who has lost part of her leg in a motorbike accident. She doesn't plan to get on a horse ever again. In the meantime, The Saddle Club and Emily are riding so much, they're saddle sore! Is it possible to get too much of a good thing?

Read all The Saddle Club **Super Editions** by Bonnie Bryant! Each one is packed full of extra action. . . .

#1 A SUMMER WITHOUT HORSES

When Stevie can't ride for a while, Lisa and Carole make a pact not to ride until their friend has recovered. After all, they're The Saddle Club, and they always stick together. To seal the pact, the girls decide that if any of them breaks the vow, they'll have to ask stuck-up Veronica diAngelo to join their club. That'll keep them out of the saddle for sure!

But can three horse-crazy girls really stay away from horses and riding for more than a day? Find out in this super edition, which contains three separate stories about Lisa, Stevie, and Carole—and their summer without horses.

#2 THE SECRET OF THE STALLION

It's going to be the most amazing Saddle Club adventure ever! The girls are traveling to horsey old England. They'll ride in a show on the grounds of a real castle. Lisa has done some homework and discovered an ancient unsolved mystery about the duke who once lived there. The duke buried treasure under the stall of his spirited stallion. Then tragedy struck—the barn burned down, and the stallion perished. A year later the duke's body was found on the same spot, his hand clutching a single fire opal. . . . Legend says the treasure will be found by a rider with fire in his heart.

The girls are busy with the show, sight-seeing in London, and getting ready for a costume ball at the castle. On that night, it seems that almost anything could happen—but the story of the duke, his stallion, and the tragedy of the burning barn couldn't replay itself, could it?

#3 WESTERN STAR

The girls can't wait for winter break from school. Carole, Stevie, and Lisa are heading West to spend the first part of their vacation at one of their favorite places—the Bar None Ranch.

But what they thought would be a quick trip turns into a snowbound adventure. The girls must rescue a herd of horses that face a terrible fate. . . .

Join The Saddle Club on an unforgettable journey that recalls the true spirit of giving and the strength of friendship.

#4 DREAM HORSE

Stevie Lake gets conked on the head so hard she's laid up in the hospital. Then she starts having weird dreams about herself and her Saddle Club friends, Carole Hanson and Lisa Atwood. No big deal—until the dreams start coming true! First it's just little things. Stevie *saw* Phil get thrown from Teddy before it happened. She *knew* Starlight was going to stomp on Carole's foot. Then Carole and Lisa rely on one of Stevie's dreams to pull a prank on stable snob Veronica diAngelo.

But when their sick friend has a scary vision, the girls aren't sure they want to know: Is it just a horse in Stevie's dreams, or is it a nightmare?

Coming in June, a brand-new
Saddle Club adventure

Carole Hanson, Stevie Lake, Lisa Atwood, and their
friend Emily are off to spend a week at one of their
favorite places: the Bar None Ranch. A whole week
of nothing but riding—The Saddle Club can't wait.
But is it possible for even these horse-crazy girls to
spend too much time in the saddle?

Turn the page for a preview of Saddle Club #66,
Saddle Sore. Then look for it in your bookstore to find
out!

"LOOK! YOU CAN see the mountains!" Emily Williams leaned forward, pressing her face against the pane of one of the plane's small windows. "Some of them even still have snow."

"The Bar None isn't that high up," Emily's friend Lisa Atwood assured her. "We won't be riding through snow."

Emily sat back. "That's good, I guess, since I only brought summer clothes. But riding through snow is fun!"

"Riding through sagebrush is fun, too," a third friend, Carole Hanson, said.

"Well, I don't know about riding *through* sagebrush," joked the final girl in the cabin, Stevie Lake. "Riding *near* sagebrush, maybe. Riding around it. Riding past it and admiring the sagebrush—that's fun. But riding *through* sagebrush hurts! It's prickly."

"I'll write that down so I don't forget it," Emily said dryly. The others laughed. It was hard for them all not to laugh, when they knew they were on their way to having such a great time riding at the Bar None ranch.

Lisa, Carole, and Stevie had been best friends for a very long time. They were all completely horse-crazy, and, in fact, they had met at Pine Hollow, a riding stable in Willow Creek, Virginia, where they all rode. When they discovered how much they had in common, they formed The Saddle Club. Its only two rules were that members had to help each other out, and they had to be totally, irredeemably, horse-crazy.

They hadn't known Emily Williams for that long, but already she was one of their close friends. Because she had cerebral palsy, Emily rode at the Free Rein Therapeutic Riding Center, a place for disabled riders. She was a very good rider. She even had her own horse, a loving palomino named P.C. Sometimes Emily came to Pine Hollow to ride, but she kept P.C. at Free Rein.

"You won't believe it, Emily," Carole said, her dark

eyes shining with excitement. "The land is so open—you won't see a fence for miles."

"Oh, please," Stevie retorted. "The only way she won't see fence is if she shuts her eyes. Em, they keep the horses in paddocks close to the barns, just the way you'd expect. They've got a little pasture for grazing, too, next to the ranch house, and they've got wire fences strung around the whole property. Otherwise the cows could just mosey into town."

"And Mrs. Devine's garden is fenced, too," Lisa remembered.

"Otherwise the cows would eat lettuce for lunch," Stevie said.

"Please!" Carole said, aiming a firm smile at Stevie. "You know what I mean, and Emily does, too. Of course there are fences. There just don't *seem* to be any. We can ride for miles, and if we ride in the right direction, there's nothing to stop us at all."

"Except a nasty bunch of sagebrush," Stevie murmured, and they all laughed. Of the three Saddle Club members, Stevie was the most playful, and she loved all sorts of jokes. Stevies's plans often landed them all in hot water, but her cleverness just as often bailed them out.

"So if my horse bucks me off, it'll be able to run for miles," Emily said. "You're right, Carole, that is something to look forward to." She said it with a laugh, and the others laughed in response.

Emily's personality was a lot like Stevie's. Both liked to have fun, but both could be incredibly stubborn. Emily's stubbornness often worked to her advantage—she kept trying a thing until she did it.

"A Bar None horse would never buck a rider off," Carole protested. "Wait until you meet them, Emily. They're the sweetest horses in the world."

If the others were horse-crazy, Carole was horse-berserk. Someday, her friends were sure, Carole would do great things in the horse world, but for now she contented herself with learning every single thing possible about them and spending all of her free time around them.

"Better than P.C.?" Emily asked. "Better than Starlight?" Starlight was Carole's own horse.

"Well, no, of course not," Carole amended. "But aside from P.C. and Starlight, they're the sweetest horses—"

"What about Belle?" Stevie demanded, at the same time as Lisa said, "What about Prancer?" Belle was Stevie's horse; Prancer was the lesson horse Lisa usually rode.

"Sorry," Carole said. "Okay, aside from P.C., Starlight, Belle, and Prancer—"

"What about Topside?" Stevie asked. Lisa added, "What about Delilah?" Both were favorite Pine Hollow horses.

Emily laughed. So did Carole. "I guess you'd better just say they have very sweet horses at the Bar None," Emily said.

"That's right," Carole said. "I'd better not draw comparisons. I couldn't anyway. Horses are all so different, like people."

"Emily, you'll love it," Lisa said softly. She was the quietest and most academic member of The Saddle Club. "I remember the first time I came to the Bar None. I really hadn't been riding for very long then, and I had never imagined a place like it."

"I have," Emily replied. "I've been dreaming and daydreaming about this trip ever since I learned we were going." Then she laughed again and tossed back her short dark hair. "I have to admit, I think Pine Hollow is pretty close to heaven, because of all the trails! It's hard to believe that this place will be even better. And I *can't* believe I'm here on this plane with you guys. It's amazing."

"Colonel Devine wanted to thank you," Carole said. "He told us you helped him a lot."

The Devines owned the Bar None and ran it as a dude ranch. Colonel Frank Devine was one of Carole's father's friends. His daughter, Kate, had first been Carole's good friend; now she was an auxiliary member of The Saddle Club. Colonel Devine had been a pilot in the military and still did some flying for corporations out West. Whenever he came to the East Coast, he tried to arrange a get-together for Kate and the Saddle Club.

The Bar None had become a popular vacation spot for families. Last spring Colonel Devine had called Carole to explain that he wanted to expand their facilities. Many of his former Marine Corps buddies were veterans of the Vietnam War, and a number of them were disabled. He wanted them to be able to enjoy the ranch, too, so he was taking steps to make the Bar None accessible to everyone. Kate had told him about The Saddle Club's work at Free Rein and the friend they had made there. Could he talk to Emily?

Carole had given him Emily's phone number, and later Emily had told her they'd had a long conversation. Frank Devine had already been in touch with several national organizations for the disabled, she said, including the North American Riding for the Handicapped Organization, or NARHA, which oversaw therapeutic riding organizations. But he had some specific questions to ask a rider, and she'd been able to answer most of them. A few months later, he'd invited them all West for a week, including Emily. Colonel Devine was flying the small plane they were in now, taking them to Kate and the ranch.

"He wanted to thank me, but he said he wants to get some work out of me, too," Emily said. "He wants my opinion on his improvements." She grinned. "This is going to be really fun."

"Passengers, prepare for landing." Colonel Devine's voice was stern over the intercom.

Emily giggled. "Does he always sound like that?"

Stevie nodded. "When he's flying, he becomes this whole other person, Colonel Invincible, Captain of the Skies. Don't worry. At the Bar None he's a regular Dad."

"He seemed regular before the plane took off," Emily said.

They gathered the books and snacks they'd spread about the small cabin and zipped their backpacks closed. Emily fit the cuffs of her crutches over her forearms. To walk she needed both crutches and leg braces, but to ride horses she didn't need either. She had a wheelchair, but she avoided using it whenever she could.

When the little plane landed, Colonel Devine had no sooner dropped the ramp down when a tall girl came flying up it. "Stevie!" she shrieked. "Carole! Lisa! *Emily!*" She gave them each a hug, nearly knocking Emily down.

"Kate!" they all shrieked back.

"Come on, let's go!" Kate said, grabbing backpacks and hurrying them out the door. "My mom's in the truck, she's dying to meet you, Emily. We brought snacks in case you're hungry, and John says hi to all of you. If we get back quickly we can ride before dinner, and, oh, Carole, wait until you see the new foals!" Kate clattered down the ramp.

Emily burst out laughing. "You're right, Carole," she said. "You said I'd feel like I knew her right away, and I do. Who's John?"

"He works at the Bar None—he and his dad. He's our age." Lisa's eyes were shining. She liked John Brightstar quite a lot. They all did, but Lisa liked him the most.

Emily made her way slowly and carefully down the ramp. None of The Saddle Club offered to help her, and neither, they noted with satisfaction, did Kate. Emily was very firm about doing things for herself.

Before long they were all on the way to the ranch. The drive was barely long enough to exchange all the news with Kate. Before long they were talking about horses.

"This is P.C." Emily pulled a photograph out of her backpack. "I knew you'd want to see what he looked like, so I brought this. It's his summer coat, fortunately. In winter he looks like a yellow bear."

"He's adorable!" Kate said. "Look how nice his expression is."

"He's perfect for me," Emily said. "He tries to do everything I ask."

"Emily even taught him to lie down on command," Stevie bragged. "She uses it for mounting and dismounting whenever there isn't a ramp around." Emily couldn't lift her foot high enough to mount a horse from the ground.

Emily grinned. "We all taught him that, Stevie, and it was your idea in the first place. But he does it whenever I need him to."

"Well, we haven't got any lying-down horses at the ranch yet," Kate said. "Moonglow does most other things, though. I can't make up my mind what sort of horse I want her to be, so right now I've got her jumping logs, schooling trot extensions and collections, working on spins."

The others laughed. Trot extensions and collections were advanced English-style riding; spins were advanced Western. "What sort of saddle are you riding her in?" Carole asked.

Kate shrugged. "Usually Western, but sometimes English."

"I didn't think you were jumping much out here," Lisa added.

Kate shrugged again, this time with a wide grin. "You see a log, you might as well jump it," she said. "Moonglow seems to think so, too." Kate had gotten Moonglow from a government sale of wild horses. Moonglow's training had been an extensive project that Kate thoroughly enjoyed. Before her parents bought the ranch, Kate had been a top competitive junior rider, but her drive to win had taken all the fun out of riding for her. She'd given it up entirely, until she met The Saddle Club; now she rode strictly for fun.

"We'll have to see some logs, then," Carole said. She loved jumping. "Kate, we came to an agreement on the plane. Emily's never ridden in a place like this, and we haven't been here for a long time. So we're going to ride all week long."

Kate looked surprised. "Do you ever do anything else?"

"Well, sometimes—"

"This week we're not doing *anything* but riding," Stevie cut in.

"Ride, ride, ride," Lisa said.

"Great!" said Kate.

Emily grinned. Her friends could see how thrilled she was.

"So, Emily," Mrs. Devine said, over the back of the front seat, "did Frank tell you all about our improvements?"

"No, he just told me to fasten my seat belt. What's new?"

They talked for a while about the ramps added to all the buildings, for wheelchair entrance, the enlarged doorways in some of the bunkhouses, and other modifications the Devines had made. Kate told them excitedly about the retraining program she and John Brightstar had undertaken with some of the ranch saddle horses.

"We tried to do everything the people from NARHA told us about," she said. "Getting them used to the mounting ramp and being mounted from either side, getting them to move off voice and stick commands, as well as leg commands—everything. Plus, of course, making sure they're super calm. We've got two or three horses we think are completely ready, and several more are coming along.

"Emily, I'm going to give you Spot for the week. He

used to be my horse, until I got Moonglow, and he's got wonderful gaits and a great disposition. You're going to love him. He's an Appaloosa."

Emily grinned. "Thanks, Kate. I'm sure I'll love him."

"One of our mares is doing amazingly well," Kate continued. "Her name is Buttercup. I've been working with her a lot, because I want her to be ready for Monica. Monica always rides Buttercup when she comes here." Kate's voice dropped to a sad tone. "I haven't told you about Monica."

Mrs. Devine looked over the back of her seat again. "Such a tragedy. And they'll be here tomorrow."

"Who?" asked Lisa.

"Monica and her parents," Kate replied. "See, they started coming here the first year we opened the ranch, and they loved it so much they came back every year. Monica's our age. She's funny and athletic, and a great rider. We got to be pretty good friends.

"She had an accident on a motorbike last fall. It crushed her lower leg, and they had to amputate it. Her parents had already made their reservations to come here. They told Mom they wanted to cancel, but Monica wouldn't let them. She wants everything in her life to be the same as it used to be."

Kate's eyes filled with tears. "I wanted to have disabled people come to the ranch, but I didn't want that to mean Monica! I mean—of course I'm glad she's coming, I'm just so sorry this happened to her."

Carole patted Kate's leg sympathetically. Lisa gave her shoulder a squeeze. "It sounds terrible," Stevie said. "We'll just have to do all we can to make sure she has a really good time."

"If she was a good rider before, she should still be a good rider," Emily said. "Does she have an artificial leg?"

Kate blinked. "I don't know."

Mr. Devine shook his head. "I don't think so. I think it's still too soon."

"That's too bad," Emily said. "What about her knee? Did they save her knee?"

Lisa burst out laughing. "Emily, what a question! You sound so practical—in a ghoulish sort of way."

Emily shook her head. "Think about it. If she still has a knee, her seat in the saddle will feel pretty normal. Otherwise it will be harder for her to balance, without an artificial leg."

"She still has her knee," Kate confirmed. "I didn't talk to her—she was still at the rehab hospital when her mother called here—but her mom said it was just her lower leg."

Emily nodded. "Good. She can use a crop for leg

commands, the way I do, but she should be able to adjust quickly. She'll be able to ride every day, just like us."

"The more the merrier," Stevie said, and the others agreed.

Win riding lessons and a saddle!

Sweepstakes sponsored by

STATE LINE TACK®
The Discount Tack Store

Hurry— enter to win!

---✂--

Return completed entry to:
Bantam Doubleday Dell, Attn: Free Riding Lessons, 1540 Broadway, 20th floor, New York, NY 10036

Name _____

Address _____

City _____ State _____ Zip _____

Date of Birth _____ / _____ / _____
                        Month   Day   Year

HORSE CRAZY SWEEPSTAKES OFFICIAL RULES